"How do you know I can't handle an affair?"

Sharon's tone was slightly belligerent. She scooted forward on the couch and looked Sam straight in the eye.

"An educated guess?" he replied after recovering from his initial shock.

Placing her hands on his shoulders, she stared at his mouth with provocative intent. "Sharon . . ." he warned as she slowly leaned forward.

"Sam," she breathed in response.

Unable and unwilling to stop her, he didn't move away when her lips descended unerringly to his. It was long, languorous minutes later when she caught his face between her hands and asked, "Do you still want to be just friends?"

"No," he replied in a husky voice. "That's not what I want at all. . . ."

Because **Janet Bieber** and
Joyce Thies both live in Ohio and,
between them, have five children, they
had plenty of inspiration for writing
A Package Deal. Once again this
talented team has created a delightfully
warm romance highlighted by humor.

Books by Jenna Lee Joyce

HARLEQUIN TEMPTATION
39–WINTERSFIELD
59–CROSSROADS
81–ONE ON ONE

These books may be available at your local bookseller.

A Package Deal

JENNA LEE JOYCE

Harlequin Books

TORONTO • NEW YORK • LONDON
AMSTERDAM • PARIS • SYDNEY • HAMBURG
STOCKHOLM • ATHENS • TOKYO • MILAN

Published June 1986

ISBN 0-373-25210-2

Printed in Canada

SAM JEFFERSON TURNED his car onto the quiet, tree-lined street, grateful to be only a few blocks from home. It had been a long trip. A week in Atlanta attending a small-town mayors' convention and then an additional week spent in Washington, D.C., as a representative of the Mayors' Association had been grueling. The exhilaration he'd felt at taking part in a roundtable discussion, held with the president of the United States in attendance, had deserted him sometime during the flight back to Ohio.

The July heat was sweltering; the last thing he'd needed when he'd retrieved his new Buick sedan from the airport parking lot was to find that the Freon in the air conditioner had either drained out or evaporated. No cooling air came from the vents, and even with the windows open, the hour's drive from Columbus to Rhodesboro seemed interminable. He'd shed his jacket and tie and rolled his shirt sleeves up to his elbows, but he was still miserable. His shirt clung to his damp skin. His black hair was wet and curling and sweat rivulets dripped down the sides of his face.

Sam hoped his ancient window unit hadn't gone the same way as the air conditioner in his car. Having been closed up for two weeks, the house was also going to seem like an oven. Even so, he couldn't wait to get home, guzzle down the cold can of beer he knew was waiting on the top shelf of his refrigerator and then duck under the cooling spray of a shower. He made a mental note to add central air conditioning to the list of renovations he was making to the carriage house he'd recently purchased.

With a smile of anticipation on his face, Sam approached the driveway that led past Diana Rhodes's large brick Victorian house to the converted carriage house at the end. Once part of the Rhodes estate, the smaller brick building was ivy covered and picturesque. Even without all the changes he envisioned, the place would cost a fortune back in suburban Chicago, Sam mused.

A slight frown furrowed his brow. The high cost of living was just one of many problems he had left behind in his other life, a life he had been determined to put behind him since moving to Rhodesboro. Three years ago, at the age of thirty-five, with one foot firmly planted on the top rung of his career ladder, he had shocked everyone by chucking all of it.

Against the advice of some of the best legal minds in Chicago, he'd abandoned his lofty political aspirations, a prestigious job, his expensive bachelor apartment overlooking Lake Michigan and a fast-paced lifestyle that was giving him ulcers. Instead of becoming the district attorney for a major metropolis, he was now a small-town mayor, a small-time lawyer and a part-time carpenter while he completed the work on his carriage house. He had never been happier.

Sam had just made the sharp right turn into the drive when something strange caught his eye. He stepped on the brakes in order to take a closer look. The rolling green lawn of the Rhodes estate, which normally boasted not one blade of grass out of place, was cluttered with overturned boxes and crates. Several bicycles reclined on their sides by the manicured shrubs that bordered the brick walkway leading to the massive front doors of the gabled house. Nerve-jarring rock music blasted from the second-story windows, and several high-pitched shrieks provided a discordant accompaniment.

"What the devil is going on here?" Sam asked out loud as he completed his turn and found he had to maneuver his sedan around a blue tricycle and a large red wagon in order to proceed.

A second later, Sam slammed on his brakes. A small yellow car was shooting backwards toward him at an alarming speed. He swerved onto the grass, grateful for his quick reflexes. The Volkswagon convertible sped on past, spewing gravel and dust in its wake.

"Sweet, bloody hell!" Sam swore as he watched the other car screech to a halt less than two yards from the wide trunk of an oak tree. He was out of his car like a shot. Striding swiftly down the drive, he was about to deliver a sound dressing-down to the maniacal driver when a woman dashed past him and beat him to it.

"Michael Francis Markovski! Hand over those keys!" The petite woman barreled down on the tall blond youth who was slowly throwing his long legs over the unopened car door.

"We were just checking out reverse gear, Mom. Tim fixed it great, didn't he?" the young giant asked, adopting a hopeful expression. "He figured out what was wrong just by looking in the manual."

Sam halted in midstep, sensing his vitriolic speech would be superfluous. He didn't know who they were or why they were in his driveway, but it was clear that the short, curly-haired brunette who was poking a finger in the teenage hulk's chest was the boy's irate mother. If the woman's stiff spine and bristling demeanor were any indication, one Michael Francis Markovski was in very deep trouble.

Sam's initial anger drained away as he perused the situation. He could even feel a measure of sympathy for the young man. He'd done his fair share of tearing around in cars when he'd been that age.

The tall, muscled youth towered over his petite mother but even so, he sheepishly dropped a set of keys into her outstretched palm. "Don't you ever back out of a driveway like that again," she lectured. "You're lucky you didn't smash into that man's car. You all could have been killed!"

Large brown eyes spitting fire, she continued sharply. "Now you can turn around, march right into the house and wait for me. We'll discuss how long it'll be before you drive again when I get there!"

"Aw, Mom," Michael complained, but was immediately cut off.

"Don't 'aw, Mom,' me, young man. And before you go anywhere you're going to apologize to this man for your negligence." That said, the woman turned her attention to the smaller youth who was still seated in the passenger seat of the small car. "Timothy James, I've got a few words for you, too."

Sam guessed the second boy was the condemned driver's younger brother although there was little resemblance between them. Timothy had curly chestnut hair like his mother's and the same overlarge brown eyes and small, almost delicate features. He was much slighter and shorter than the other boy, but the cowed expression on their faces was identical.

"Tim, you're not blameless, so you'll be joining our discussion." She tossed him the keys. "Drive this thing forward, and put it back in the garage."

"Yes, ma'am," Timothy acknowledged respectfully, though shocked surprise widened his eyes. In a flash he maneuvered his gangly body over the gearshift and onto the driver's seat. With a grind of gears that made Sam wince on behalf of the transmission, the car lurched forward.

"Slowly, Tim," the mother warned. She stood with her hands on her denim-clad hips and watched as the boy drove the convertible at a jerky snail's pace back in the direction it had just come. Only when she was satisfied that he had safely maneuvered past the silver sedan, did she turn around to face Sam and Michael.

"Michael..." she prompted.

"Ah... er," the youth stammered, his blue eyes downcast as he approached Sam. Then manfully, he lifted his head and looked Sam straight in the face. "Sorry about what happened, sir," he apologized, working hard to keep his newly acquired baritone at a low pitch. "It won't happen again, I promise."

Michael extended his hand to seal the vow he'd just made. Then he added as if it explained everything, "I'm Mike Markovski, and, um, like we weren't expecting anybody in the driveway."

Sam grasped the offered hand, impressed by the firm handshake but dismayed that his own palm was swallowed up in the boy's huge paw. "I'm Sam Jefferson, Mike. I wasn't expecting anyone, either."

"And I'm Sharon Markovski, this rascal's mother," the woman supplied, coming to her son's side.

She also extended her hand in greeting, and Sam found himself thoroughly enjoying the feel of her small slender palm. Perhaps his pleasure was so great because his fingers were no longer in the bruising clutches of the golden bear. Whatever, he realized he was holding on to the feminine hand too long and reluctantly let go.

"I'm Diana Rhodes's niece," Sharon clarified after waving Michael toward the house. "And I'm afraid we're your new neighbors."

With effort, Sam stopped himself from blurting out his surprise. The quick mind that had proved a bonus in sizing up an opponent in the courtroom and recalling all the facts in lengthy legal briefs held him in good stead. In the space of a few seconds, he recalled every tidbit of information he'd ever heard about Sharon Markovski.

The venerable Diana Rhodes, his closest neighbor and Rhodesboro's leading citizen, had made a few passing references to a niece whose husband had died and left her with five children to support. Strong willed as she was, Diana had been frustrated by the woman's stubborn refusal to accept any financial assistance or give up her home in Pittsburgh. Evidently, circumstances had changed.

Somehow, Sharon Markovski wasn't exactly what Sam had expected the tenacious-sounding niece to be. She was a gorgeous, doe-eyed brunette with a flawless peaches-and-cream complexion, cute pixie nose and a slim, softly curved figure that sent his blood racing.

"I'm happy to meet you, Mrs. Markovski," he stated sincerely.

With a disbelieving laugh that he found delightful she said, "I'm sure me and mine are about as welcome as the plague, but I admire your good manners, Mr. Jefferson." Sharon's brown eyes twinkled with humor, and a pair of entrancing dimples caught his attention.

"I cannot tell a lie," Sam said, matching her tone. "You and yours certainly aren't what I would have expected. But, so far, with the exception of a momentary fear for my life, I can find no fault with my new neighbors."

Based on circumstantial evidence, Sam admitted, he had conceived an image of the Markovski clan, thus breaking a cardinal rule of the law. For one thing, he had assumed her children would not only be young but small, definitely not bigger and taller than he was. Just shy of six feet, Sam thought himself in pretty good shape for his thirty-eight years, but standing next to Michael, he'd felt considerably older, weaker and much more humble than he had prior to their meeting.

His reaction to the boy's mother was equally out of character. He wanted to impress her. Forgetting his fatigue, Sam felt a juvenile urge to puff out his chest and strut his stuff. That was an attitude he couldn't recall having adopted with a female since he'd been about the age of this woman's son.

"So you've moved in with your aunt," he stated the obvious.

"I'm afraid so." Sharon had to give the man credit. He was doing a good job of covering his shock, but it was there all the same. She saw it in the sharp rise of his slashing brows, the slight drop of his sensual lower lip and the barely discernable sucking in of an already flat belly.

She hoped she'd been just as skillful at masking her reaction and surprise upon meeting him. All Aunt Di had told her about the man who'd bought the carriage house was that he'd been a high-powered Chicago attorney who'd retired to the slower pace of the small town about three years prior. He'd established a legal practice and had quickly earned a reputation for honesty and straightforwardness. A descendant of one of Rhodesboro's founding fathers, he had followed in his family's footsteps and been elected mayor in the last election.

Sharon hadn't given the man much thought, and if Aunt Di had ever described him, she hadn't been paying attention. She'd assumed he was close to her aunt's age and had even toyed with the idea of doing a little matchmaking. However, standing before her was a sophisticated man who would need no help finding a woman. And he was at least two decades too young for Sharon's sixty-five-year-old maiden aunt. She most certainly hadn't expected someone with the exalted name of Samuel Adams Jefferson to be so good-looking, so . . . virile.

The feminine vanity that had made her get her figure back after the births of each of the children was now making her wish she was meeting this handsome ebony-haired man under more favorable conditions.

What with her eldest child nearly crashing into his expensive car, and she in turn screaming like a banshee, theirs had hardly been the most auspicious meeting. But then, she wasn't out to foster any relationship with him other than neighbor. She had her hands full with two half-grown males and a trio of daughters without worrying about the impression she was making on him. Though she wished she didn't look such a mess.

She was wearing a pair of cutoffs that had once belonged to Michael, a faded old blouse tied in a knot beneath her breasts, was bare-footed and didn't have on a lick of makeup. Appropriate and comfortable attire for unpacking but not for meeting a suave man like this—and a mayor to boot. He had every right to exercise his executive authority and take out an ordinance against them. Based on what he'd seen of them so far, it was obvious the community had gone on a downhill slide when the Markovski mob had moved in.

In an effort to gauge the shock of introducing the rest of her rambunctious family, she boldly asked, "Aunt Di didn't prepare you for us, did she?"

Unwittingly, when she looked straight up into his lean face and focused directly on his gray eyes, she gave him one of her "you better come clean, buster" looks. It was a look her children were very familiar with, and had so labeled behind her back. It demanded immediate compliance.

Sharon was surprised when Sam's eyes shifted away from hers for a second before he returned her gaze and a sheepish grin came up on his lips.

"How much preparation am I going to need?" he inquired smoothly.

Sharon was taken aback by the sensual undertone in his voice. For a second she'd allowed herself to think that he wasn't nearly as worldly and sophisticated as she'd first judged. She swiftly went back to her original estimation, especially when she felt his admiring gaze cataloging her physical assets in a way that quickened her breathing and made her feel very young, gauche and inexperienced.

Everything about Sam Jefferson screamed money, power and breeding. His cheekbones created aristocratic planes on his face. His perfectly sculpted cap of black hair had just the right touch of silver at the temples. His eyes snapped with intelligence. His manners were impeccable and his clothing, wilted as it was, shouted the name of a fine tailor.

She wondered what on earth he was doing practicing law in a little burg in the middle of Ohio farmland. And why in the world he was looking at her as if she was the type of woman he'd like to take to bed.

"I have five kids," Sharon pointed out, using the words as a shield to protect herself from his heated gaze. "Aunt Di neglected to mention that when she told you we were coming to live here, didn't she?"

"On the contrary," Sam negated truthfully. *She just didn't tell me you were a gorgeous little beauty and your kids were practically grown.* "She mentioned your family a long time ago, but didn't tell me much about you."

"That's understandable. The less said the better." Sharon smiled ruefully. She looked past him to the majestic oak trees that shaded the lawn and the driveway, took in the two graceful old houses across the street and their neatly clipped yards. "The old neighborhood will never be the same."

"Pittsburgh's loss is Rhodesboro's gain," Sam declared diplomatically. "As mayor, let me extend an official welcome to our little town," he offered with apparent civic pride, then with a wry smile amended, "Or, should I say welcome home, Miss Rhodes?"

Sharon laughed in response to his flirtatious grin, feeling younger and more carefree than she had in a long time. "I haven't been called Miss Rhodes in years, and I can't claim Rhodesboro as my home since I wasn't even born here.

"Though I must admit Aunt Di and my father instilled in me a great deal of pride in my name. It's exciting to think that one of my ancestors had the courage and principles to fight for his freedom. It took real grit to come out to the wilderness and carve out a piece of civilization."

Laughing lightly, Sam teased, "You sound like the president of the Rhodesboro Women's Heritage League."

"I suppose that's one of the groups Aunt Di will expect me to join now that I'm an official Rhodesboro resident," Sharon said thoughtfully, then turned the conversation to him. "How about you? Aren't you a descendent of the Jefferson who helped settle this town and then founded the college?"

"Yes, but I'm not going to join the League," he quipped.

"Why not?" she challenged in mock innocence, dimples flashing mischievously.

"I would hope the reason would be obvious," Sam returned, a very masculine grin across his face.

"Don't let your sex stop you," Sharon taunted playfully, the inherited fire of a revolutionary glinting in her eyes. "Doesn't your name reflect your ancestry and give some indication of the kind of person you are? I should think you'd be willing to make a stand for male equality, represent Rhodesboro's men in the Heritage League—Samuel Adams Jefferson."

Sam winced. "Diana told you my full name?" At her nod, he confessed, "I've suffered no small amount of teasing because of that handle. Your aunt is one of the few people in town who knows it, and I'd appreciate it if it stayed that way."

"Why? Aren't you a firebrand for independence like your namesake?"

"Hardly," Sam scoffed in self-derision. "I haven't instigated a single revolution or penned any documents that will change the course of human events."

Shoving his hands in his pockets, Sam crossed his legs at the ankles, leaned against the fender of his car and grinned. "How about you, Mrs. Markovski? Do you credit your heroic ancestor, General Rhodes, with the fighting spirit I saw you exhibit with your son today? I don't know if I'd have had the courage to tangle with that giant."

Sharon tried not to gawk like a star-struck teenager at the way the summer-weight fabric of his gray suit straightened across his belly and thighs. No way would Sam Jefferson ever pass the Heritage League's gender requirement, but he probably wouldn't have any trouble at all convincing that bastion of conservatism to accept him as its first male member.

Just then he breathed deeply, his chest expanding and straining the buttons of his fitted white shirt to give her an tantalizing glimpse of the smooth, tanned skin beneath. The shirt was unbuttoned partway down his chest, revealing a wedge of dark hair that further proclaimed his sex. Sharon marveled that Sam had the same whipcord-hard body as some of the popular singers her thirteen-year-old daughter, Merry, was always mooning over.

Come to think of it, she hadn't felt this warm and trembly inside since she'd been about Merry's age. Then the male physique had been a total mystery and the object of great fascination. But after so many years of marriage, years of familiarity with a male body, Sharon certainly hadn't expected to feel that way again. Ever. She didn't quite know what to make of it.

Suddenly she realized that she wasn't holding up her end of the conversation. She struggled to remember what Sam had just asked her, something about her "fighting spirit." Desperate to fill the silence, she spouted the first cliché that came to mind. "Right makes might."

With a cheeky grin, she held up her fist in a gesture of power. "Besides I've never told Michael I'm much smaller than he is, and he doesn't appear to have noticed."

"He won't hear it from me," Sam promised solemnly, but his lips were twitching with suppressed laughter.

The reference to her eldest reminded Sharon that she had two sons waiting for a well-deserved lecture. "I'd better go and have a serious talk with my up-and-coming Indy 500 driver and his head mechanic. Sorry about the reckless driving, and thanks for being a heads-up driver."

She started walking away, then stopped and looked over her shoulder. "I hope you have a good sense of humor and, uh, maybe you'd better buy a set of ear-plugs. You're going to need 'em."

"MICHAEL SAYS you've met our neighbor," Diana Rhodes stated as Sharon entered the kitchen.

"Almost head-on," Sharon muttered wearily, smiling her thanks as her aunt handed her a tall glass of iced tea. "Heaven help the poor man," she said under her breath when she heard the sound of tires crunching on the graveled driveway as Sam drove past the main house. She dropped onto one of the benches flanking the long harvest table.

The vivacity she'd displayed with Sam had evaporated as soon as she'd mounted the back steps. Insecurity about the rightness of the decisions she'd made and continued making for her children overshadowed all other emotions. Maybe it had been a mistake to up-root them and bring them to Rhodesboro. They'd been here only a week, and already the boys were at loose ends.

No, she reminded herself grimly. In Pittsburgh, she'd been locked into a low-paying, dead-end job, barely able to make ends meet. For the past year, in order to keep their heads above water, she'd been forced to work long hours of overtime. She could have gone on that way but would have had to deal with the constant worry over the effect her absence from home was having on the children.

When both Michael and Merry developed disciplin-3ary problems at school, Sharon realized she could expect more of the same if their situation didn't change, so she'd made her decision. Swallowing her pride, she'd finally accepted her aunt's invitation to move to Rhodesboro. Her only other choice would have been to accept the financial aid offered by her parents, who had never approved of the man she married, and suffer the "I told you so" attitude they'd no longer attempted to hide since the death of Mike, Sr. At least her aunt had admired and appreciated Mike for his hard work and devotion to her.

Yes, the move to Rhodesboro had been a wise one. Still, her children were city kids born and bred. They might have trouble adjusting to life in such a small town. And there might be new problems she would be called upon to handle.

Sharon took a long, cooling swallow of her tea and forced the familiar questions and doubts out of her mind. Over the rim of the glass, she glared at her two sons who were lounging against the counter. In no-nonsense terms she delivered a speech on responsibility and safety, ending with, "You two will spend the rest of the day at hard labor. You can start bv weeding Aunt Di's garden."

The sentence was met by a duet of adolescent groans that was completely ignored. "When you're done there, report back to me. And, Michael, you're confined to foot power until further notice. After this stunt you're going to have to demonstrate that you can handle a car in a responsible manner. That means you'll spend a week with me in the passenger seat making sure you haven't forgotten what you learned in driver's training."

Michael opened his mouth to complain but thought better of it when he saw his mother's narrowed eyes and the firm set of her mouth. Without a word, the boys rose from the table and trudged to the door. No sooner had the screen door closed behind them than the swinging door leading to the dining room crashed into the wall.

"Mom, she's done it again," Merry stormed, her blue eyes sparking with outrage.

Four-year-old Dee Dee was right behind her, her cherub face screwed up in indignation. "I didn't neither. I didn't do it."

Merry spun around and shouted, "Yes you did, you little brat!"

"Uh-uh," Dee Dee insisted, seeking refuge on her mother's lap.

"What's this all about?" Sharon asked, prying Dee Dee's chubby arms from around her neck and addressing her thirteen-year-old daughter, the apparent victim of some monumental crime.

"She's always getting into my stuff, and I'm sick of it. This time she wrecked Duran Duran," Merry wailed, her bottom lip quivering as she held back tears. "I spent my whole allowance on it, and she ruined it." Further details were lost in a barrage of semihysterical accusations.

Picking out the few words that made sense, Sharon was able to determine that a tape of Merry's favorite rock group had jammed and unreeled while Dee Dee was playing Merry's portable stereo without permission. In Merry's eyes, this was a sin of tremendous magnitude and called for capital punishment.

Sharon's suggestion that Merry try to unravel the tape from the player and rewind it on its reel was met with a begrudging agreement to try and a plea that Dee Dee be forbidden to enter her room ever again. "I need a lock," Merry maintained, her delicate features conveying a surprisingly belligerent appearance. "Just because she's the baby, she thinks she can do whatever she wants. All she's got to do is start crying, and you let her get away with murder."

"I know you're upset, Merry, but ruining a tape isn't that great a crime." Even as she said it, Sharon had to agree that there was some justification to Merry's remarks. Dee Dee was already well into her act. The tears and sniffles that had started quietly had now escalated to loud caterwauling. A newcomer to the scene would have thought Dee Dee was the plaintiff instead of the accused.

"That will be enough, Miss Bernhardt," Sharon admonished her youngest, seeing through the heavy drama. Patience wearing thin, she lifted Dee Dee off her lap and gave her daughter a gentle nudge toward the stairs. "I think you both could settle this in a more civilized manner. Dee Dee, stay out of Merry's room, and Merry, don't be so quick to demand blood. Dee Dee shouldn't have been playing with your stereo, but she didn't ruin your tape on purpose."

Hands on hips, Sharon stood at the base of the stairs until she heard the bedroom doors close overhead. She listened for any renewal of active hostilities. Satisfied that a fragile peace had been restored, she turned back to the table. "I'm sorry, Aunt Di."

"For what?" the older woman asked as she pulled a tray of cookies from the oven. The simple domestic task seemed very much out of character for the chairman of the board of the Rhodesboro Bank. Sharon was once again reminded that Diana Rhodes had many sides to her character. Still, she had to bite back a smile at the sight of her tall, aristocratic aunt, a flour smudge on her aquiline nose, wiping her beringed, manicured fingers on the long cobbler's apron that covered her expensive dress.

"I'm sorry for all the noise, the fights, the chaos—" She paused to scoop up two pairs of filthy tennis shoes from the floor and a discarded sweatshirt from the counter. She added them to an assortment of other soiled garments accumulating in a laundry basket near the basement stairs.

"The clutter," she continued. "It was sweet of you to ask us to move in, but I'll understand if you've changed your mind. Today, the real Markovski children have shown up. Those polite, well-behaved kids who've been hanging around here all week were fakes."

"Thank heavens," Diana said blithely, pushing an errant strand of silver-streaked auburn hair back in place. Her blue eyes snapped with laughter. "I wondered how long they'd keep up that act. It was unnatural. I'd say they're finally feeling at home, wouldn't you?"

"Too much so," Sharon agreed, totally disgruntled. "You couldn't have known what you were getting into. We're bringing nothing but turmoil into your well-ordered life."

"Well-ordered and dull as yesterday's mashed potatoes," Diana retorted. "My life has become so tidy and scheduled, it's a wonder I've got a brain left. I'm not much better than Pavlov's dogs, salivating every time I hear a bell. I just look at the day of the week and go to the appropriate meeting.

"There was nothing sweet about my asking you to move here. It was a totally selfish decision," she asserted, scooping the hot cookies to a cooling rack on the counter. "I'm all alone and pretty boring company."

"Oh come on," Sharon scoffed. "You're the most interesting person I've ever known. You've traveled all over the world. Your life's so exciting. I'm envious."

"Travel journals and photo albums aren't good company, and I've begun to identify with all the old ruins and relics I've tripped over in recent years. There's nothing to envy about an old woman who can recite Fodor's guides by rote."

Dropping teaspoonfuls of batter on the cookie sheet, Diana went on to say, "Your great-grandfather didn't build this monstrosity of a house for one old soul to rattle around in. It was meant for a large family, but my generation didn't do their part. Your father moved away and I was too picky about finding the right man to help me fill it with children when I was young. I'm absolutely delighted to have you and your beautiful family living here now."

Not giving Sharon a chance to respond, Diana repeated the arguments she'd used to persuade Sharon to sell the house in Pittsburgh and move to Ohio. "I know that you and the children would have managed, but it would have been just that. There is no sense in your scraping along when you can live here free in a house that'll be yours someday anyway."

Diana slid the sheet of cookies into the oven and closed the door. After setting the timer, she turned to Sharon with a gentle smile. "Mike, bless his memory, worked so hard to give you and the children a good life. Maybe he was a little shortsighted in not having more life insurance but that's the optimism of youth. He'd never have wanted you and the children to suffer from that mistake. Save the money from the house to provide the education he wanted for his children."

Sharon blinked back the tears of gratitude she felt for her aunt's support of Mike. Diana had always seen his special qualities, understood why Sharon had fallen in love with him. Still, though her aunt kept constantly reassuring her that their coming was no burden, financial or otherwise, Sharon felt it only right that she assume her share of the responsibility.

"But you're not even letting me pay any of the living expenses, Aunt Di," she reminded. "I should get a part-time job. Feeding Michael alone could break you."

"No part-time job," Diana pronounced firmly. "Going to school and being a mother is enough for anybody to have to do at one time. The deal is you get your education while I house, feed and clothe the kids. You've got only one more year before you get your degree. Once you have a teaching position, we'll talk about a new arrangement, okay?"

"Do I have a choice?"

"None."

After sliding the last tray of cookies out of the oven, Diana joined her niece at the table. During their discussion Sharon had attacked the mountain of clean socks heaped at one end of the table and had spread two long lines of singles on the planked wood. Diana chose a sock from the pile and placed it on its mate as if playing a game of solitaire.

The two women worked together wordlessly for a while until the strains of a Bach "Inventio," being played on the old reed organ, drifted into the kitcen. "I wondered where Theresa was," Sharon remarked absently.

"She's been holed up in the library with my old set of encyclopedias," Diana supplied as she held up a red striped athletic sock and looked for its mate. "What a thirsty mind that child has."

"Well, don't let it get around that she reads the encyclopedia for fun," Sharon remarked. "That kid'll have enough problems finding friends without them knowing what she likes to do with her free time. Most eleven-year-old girls don't consider reference books light reading."

Diana laughed, a booming laugh that filled the room and would have surprised many of Rhodesboro's conservative citizens had they heard it. "You've brought life to this old mausoleum," she said when she could control her voice.

"And you're either a saint or you're crazy," Sharon teased.

2

SAM DROPPED HIS TOWEL on the floor next to his bed. He slid between the cool sheets and settled his nude body onto the mattress. The quiet hum of the window air conditioner was a lullaby. Stretched out on his stomach, so tired he was almost numb, Sam expected sleep to envelop him within seconds.

Suddenly a blast of warring guitars bombarded the walls of the carriage house. Startled, Sam flipped over and jackknifed to an upright position. Every beat of the drums, every twang of steel strings, every crash of an electric keyboard attacked the brick structure and its outraged inhabitant. Sam's previously benumbed nerves switched into high gear and all his tendons drew taut.

"Teenagers," he reminded himself, and coaxed all his muscles to relax as he lay back, resettled himself and tried to will his body into a state of unconsciousness. It was no use. Purchasing a set of earplugs would be his top priority tomorrow morning.

He turned onto his stomach and pulled a pillow over his head. It helped. He couldn't actually hear the music any longer, but his skin continued to register the vibrations. He thought longingly of another beer, but he'd already drunk the sole occupant of his refrigerator.

He considered guzzling down the better portion of a fifth of Scotch, then discarded the idea. It might dull his brain, but it would also wreak havoc on his stomach lining. Reactivating the ulcer he'd worked so hard to heal would be a high price to pay for one afternoon's nap. A few hours of rest wasn't worth that kind of agony.

Finally, after several more tosses and turns, he was able to fall asleep. The restorative oblivion didn't last nearly long enough. The insistent buzz of his doorbell brought him up off the bed. Angrily he grabbed for his robe, belting it around his middle as he strode purposefully across the loft and climbed down the ladder to the main room. His humor didn't improve when he stubbed his toe against the pile of lumber that would one day comprise the stairs.

He had a good idea who was on the other side of his door. Mrs. Krouse, the elderly widow across the street, who, on a weekly basis, requested his assistance in coaxing her cat down from the tree behind her house. In the past he'd patiently complied, usually finding the cat already safely on the ground, licking its paws while it waited for its mistress. He had never wanted to upset the old soul by informing her that rescuing cats wasn't a mayoral duty, even if said mayor did have a handy ladder.

Today, he felt differently. As he limped across the room, he vowed that the moment he completed the stairs to the loft, the ladder was going to be chopped up into splinters.

His appearance at the door clad in nothing but a thigh-length robe would no doubt shock the lady out of her support hose, he thought with some small measure of satisfaction. The mere sight of him might be enough to discourage her. For insurance, he was going to suggest she call the animal-control warden.

Sam yanked the door open. "Mrs. Krouse, I'm—"

Nobody was there. He blinked and ran his fingers through his hair. "I must be hearing things," he mumbled to himself, and started to close the door. A gleam of copper at about knee level caught his attention. Openmouthed, he stared down at the little girl who stood smiling up at him, a plate heaped with homemade cookies in her hands.

"Hullo, Mr. Jefferson," she greeted sweetly, a smile as bright as her shining red hair beaming up at him. "I'm Dee Dee, and these are for you." She thrust the cookies toward him.

"Uh...thank you," Sam answered, grabbing the plate with both hands before it clattered to the floor. "I'm very happy to meet you, Dee Dee, and thank you for the cookies."

"You're welcome," the little girl chirped brightly.

She didn't seem inclined to say more, and Sam assumed the hospitable presentation of the still-warm baked goods was her only reason for coming. Since there appeared to be nothing more to say, he stepped back, intending to elbow the door closed, but his half-pint visitor evidently took his movement as an invitation and waltzed past him into the main room.

"Can I have a glass of milk with mine?" Dee Dee asked as she seated herself on his couch, carefully arranging the skirt of her sundress on each side of her primly crossed legs and folding her tiny hands in her lap. "If you don't got milk, Kool-Aid's okay."

Queen Victoria couldn't have been more regally commanding than the little girl seated on Sam's couch, even though her feet dangled several inches above the floor, her hair was arranged in two beribboned ponytails and her pixie face was dusted with freckles. Sam blinked in astonishment but accepted his position as her lowly subject. He couldn't think of anything else to do.

Suddenly he realized that he didn't have the slightest clue how to deal with a person of her age. In fact, he couldn't recall ever having spoken to one before. What he knew about little kids wouldn't cover the back of a postage stamp. "I'm afraid it may have to be water," he apologized as he placed the cookies on the box of books that currently served as his coffee table.

"Are you bare naked under your robe?" Dee Dee asked guilelessly, turning her sky-blue eyes up at him.

"Uh...uh...uh," Sam stammered, startled and experiencing a brief sense of panic. "I...I was asleep."

"Don't you wear jammies?"

"No, I don't," he answered uneasily, questioning his sanity for allowing this conversation to progress but finding himself, supposedly a master of communication, unable to come up with a diplomatic way to get rid of his unwanted guest. Uncomfortably, he settled himself onto a chair, careful to keep his robe arranged modestly.

"My mommy wouldn't let you do that," Dee Dee announced without a bat of an eye. "She says it's unci . . . incivi—"

"Uncivilized?"

"Uh-huh," Dee Dee agreed, and sent him a dazzling smile of appreciation for completing the word for her. "Mommy says it's that word if you don't sleep in jammies or nighties. Do you know what's a bar . . . barbarian?"

"Somebody who doesn't sleep in jammies or nighties?" Sam suggested more to himself than his guest.

Dee Dee sighed, an overly dramatic display of long-suffering. "That's right. My brothers are them."

Sam hooted with laughter, but was immediately repentant when he saw the look of confusion on the little girl's face. "I'm sorry, Dee Dee," he apologized, then changed the subject before he got into deeper trouble. "Are you the youngest Markovski?"

"I'm the baby," she pronounced proudly.

"I met your mother and your brothers a few hours ago." Sam was beginning to fidget beneath the bright eyes studying him far too intently.

"My brothers aren't hairy like you," Dee Dee declared bluntly.

Involuntarily Sam grabbed at the lapels of his robe and closed the wide vee opening as best he could. If he could have tugged the hem over his knees, he would have. In all his adult life, he'd never been so self-conscious about his state of undress. It was definitely time to ask little Miss Markovski to leave before she had him cowering in a closet to escape her blatant perusal.

The child's brow furrowed as she continued staring. Then, as if she'd made a momentous decision, she declared kindly, "It's okay. I like you anyway."

"That's a relief," Sam said sardonically, rising from the chair and tightening the belt on his robe. He intended to thank the little girl for the cookies again and wish her a good day as he hastily ushered her out the door. He smiled at her. "It's been a pleasure meeting you, Dee Dee."

"I know," she said simply, standing up.

Sam took heart, fully believing she was about to leave voluntarily.

Dee Dee brushed imaginary wrinkles from her gingham skirt, cleared her throat, and to Sam's ever-lasting surprise, burst into song.

Completely flummoxed, he sought the wall for support. Dee Dee's childish soprano took delightful license with both the melody and lyrics of "America." Sam's initial shock wore off, and with one shoulder leaning against the rough-hewed paneling, he crossed his arms over his chest, resigned to the fate of being serenaded. Whether he wanted it or not, the Markovski's were determined to bombard him with one kind of music or another. If he'd been given a choice, he'd take Dee Dee's singing over the heavy-metal beat blaring in the background.

At the song's end, Sam applauded. Dee Dee curtsied, thanked him and sat down. "I usually charge ten cents for a song, but that one was free," she informed him with aplomb.

"That's very gracious of you," Sam told her, tongue in cheek. Having long since given up any hope of returning to his nap, he started for the kitchen area. Right or wrong, he decided, the only way to treat this little girl was as an adult.

"Let me see what I have in here that we could possibly drink with those cookies. I've been gone for a while, and the cupboards might be pretty bare," he apologized as he opened and closed the cabinet doors.

The refrigerator's freezer section yielded a can of orange-juice concentrate. Sam was in the process of smashing the frozen sticky glob with a potato masher before attempting to mix it with water when he heard a rap at the door. Before he could answer it, Dee Dee had appointed herself his hostess.

"Hi, Mommy. Come on in. Me and Mr. Jefferson are having a party."

"And just who thought up this party?" Sharon asked as she stepped inside, her eyes searching for the host her daughter had drafted into service.

"It seemed the least I could do after being serenaded by such a charming songstress," Sam supplied good-naturedly, hoping his expression showed none of the relief he felt at the sight of the child's mother. At last, the cavalry had arrived to rescue him from this tiny bushwhacker.

"Do join us," he invited as he finished mixing the juice. Abruptly it struck him that he couldn't imagine anything more enjoyable than spending the next half hour or so with this mother-daughter pair, except spending an even longer time alone with the intriguing mother.

"That's very kind of you, Mr. Jefferson," Sharon began, trying to keep her gaze anywhere but where it was being drawn. Since the lower half of Sam's body was concealed behind the bar separating the kitchen from the main room, she could only guess how long his robe was, but she knew he was wearing nothing else.

For her peace of mind, Sharon hoped Sam stayed where he was until she'd ushered Dee Dee and herself out the door. The velvety gray robe matched his eyes and gaped just enough to expose a tantalizing glimpse of his marvelously masculine chest. Dee Dee had obviously summoned him from the shower, or bed.

Either place brought forth images that rocked Sharon's equilibrium. She could far too easily conjure up a picture of the bed that no doubt occupied the huge loft. In keeping with the natural decor of stone and wood evolving in the partially finished house, Sam's bedspread was probably a fur throw.

"I'm sure Dee Dee's taken up enough of your time," she offered as an excuse for escape. "I'm sorry she bothered you."

She was afraid to bring up the question of how much he had been charged for the dubious pleasure of hearing Dee Dee sing. Back in Pittsburgh, her career as a wandering minstrel had been profitable enough to enable her to purchase a jump rope and an assortment of other treasures. Obviously the imp had decided she wasn't going to suffer a financial setback because of this move to a new neighborhood.

Sam placed the pitcher of orange juice in the middle of the tray, then cocked his head to one side, listening. "It's quiet," he said in amazement and relief.

"The boys are working in the front yard now, and I made them turn down the volume," Sharon told him, then clamped a firm hand on Dee Dee's shoulder and started steering her toward the door. "We'll be going now."

"Please." Sam's voice, powerful in its melodic resonance, stayed her progress. "Don't go."

At Sharon's arrival, his comfort level had increased a hundredfold. In his dealings with adult females, at least Sam was on safe ground. Calling upon the same persuasive powers he used to charm a jury, he coaxed, "I'm looking forward to diving into those cookies, and as delicious as I'm guessing they are, they'll taste all the better if I share them with two lovely ladies."

The man had definitely won all of Rhodesboro's female vote, Sharon surmised after responding to Sam's charm and agreeing to stay. She and Dee Dee sat down on the couch. Sharon was aware that she was depending on the presence of a four-year-old for her sanity.

With Dee Dee there, she would have to control the wild sensations close proximity to this man caused in her body.

Sam placed another glass on the tray he was preparing. As he came around the bar, the tender arch of his bare foot encountered the sharp corners of the belt buckle he'd left lying on the floor. Hopping quickly onto his other foot, he miraculously kept the tray level, avoiding catastrophe while cursing himself for having left his clothes strewed all over in the first place.

Unfortunately, his high-kneed gallop placed disastrous strain on the belt holding his robe closed. When he felt the two halves of the front part company, he pivoted toward the bar, thankful that his female guests had their backs to him. He'd heard enough comments about his body for one day. He returned the tray to the safety of the butcher-block surface of the bar and grabbed the loose ends of his belt.

Looping the strip of velour securely around his waist, he then surreptitiously inched along the bar, sweeping his pants, socks and briefs along with the side of his foot. A quick kick, and the balled garments shot into the kitchenette and away from the no-doubt disapproving eyes of the woman seated on his couch. His jacket, shoes, shirt, tie and garment bag were still lying where he'd dropped them, but there wasn't too much he could do about that without scurrying around like a nervous neatnik.

Trying to make the place look totally civilized and tidy would be fruitless anyway, it being in a half-

constructed state. His tools and equipment were set up
in one corner that served as a workshop. Lumber was
stacked here and there. Crated furniture took up a good
third of the space. Only the bare necessities—one chair,
the couch, a table and his bed up in the loft were proof
that he actually lived in the midst of the construction.
Rustic, Sam decided, was the kindest description for his
dwelling.

"Here we go," he announced, placing the tray next
to the plate of cookies. "Not exactly high tea, *madame*
and *mademoiselle*," he said grandly for Dee Dee's
benefit. He winked at her and to his delight received an
exaggerated wink in return from the little blue-eyed
enchantress.

"You're a very good orange-juice maker," Dee Dee
complimented him a few minutes later when everyone
had been served.

"And these are very good," Sam returned, this time
directing his smile toward Sharon as he reached for another oatmeal cookie. "I haven't had any like this since
I was a little boy visiting my grandmother."

"Aunt Di made them from her mother's recipe. It's
the cinnamon that makes the difference." *Oh help!*
Sharon groaned inwardly. Surely she was able to think
of something more scintillating to talk about than the
ingredients of oatmeal cookies.

"Your grandmother and mine were great friends,
grew up together as I recall," Sam inserted. "Grandma
was a Fredericks, one of the Johnny-come-lately fami-
lies of Rhodesboro."

"Not exactly," Sharon corrected, grateful he'd introduced a new topic of conversation, since her brain had obviously turned to mush. "The Fredericks family arrived around the turn of the century. The town's doctor had just died along with half his patients in a flu epidemic. Dr. and Mrs. Isaiah Fredericks were welcomed with open arms."

"You're really up on this town's history, aren't you?" Admiration was clear in Sam's eyes.

A little self-consciously Sharon confided, "I'm a walking encyclopedia of useless trivia. So's my daughter Theresa."

"There's nothing useless or trivial about history, and Theresa must be as bright as her mother," Sam complimented.

"Mike says it's dumb and dull," Dee Dee inserted.

"I'm afraid your brother thinks the only important history is that of the NFL," Sharon remarked ruefully, smoothing her hand over Dee Dee's shining red bangs. "I'll have to try a little harder to make history come alive for him."

"Were you a history major in college?" Sam asked.

"Er...ah...no," Sharon answered uneasily. "I'm still working to get my degree in elementary education. I've transferred to Jefferson for my senior year. Majoring in history didn't seem too practical. I read it for pleasure and take as many electives in the subject as I can."

Cursing himself for putting her on the defensive, Sam let her know he admired her choice and most of all her drive to complete her education. After a few minutes he knew he'd succeeded in making her more comfortable when she began to talk at length about her enrollment at the University of Pittsburgh as a part-time student. She made no mention of more recent years, and Sam guessed she'd had to put her education on hold when her husband had died.

It was more what she left out than what she said that gave Sam a good idea of the life she'd led since her marriage. She'd been very young, had given birth to her first four children in the space of five years and still had the determination to get a college degree. Sam couldn't help but admire her pluck.

"The chance to finish up my schooling was one of the enticements for moving to Rhodesboro," Sharon stated enthusiastically, though she was trying to find a suitable opening to switch the subject and stop the conversation from being so one-sided.

Sam's encouragement and interest in her studies had to be prompted by the good breeding she'd credited him with upon first acquaintance. Unfortunately, she'd not been able to discuss her college courses or her love of history with her husband without fearing she'd dent his fragile ego. Mike had always been half-afraid she might leave him in favor of someone who was more her social and intellectual equal. This man would suffer no such qualms.

Sam exuded self-confidence. Sitting a few feet away from her, clad in nothing but a bathrobe, he was remarkably at ease. Even more amazing, he'd put her at ease. Though she still maintained a purely red-blooded appreciation of his gorgeous body, she'd somehow managed to control her reactions.

Somewhere in the midst of their conversation, her nerves had stopped standing on end every time he spoke. She'd even been able to string words together without pausing to gulp and gape at the sinewy, hair-covered legs stretched out a few feet away from her. The room afforded plenty of other places for her gaze to wander. A magnificent stone fireplace, the beautiful paneling installed at a forty-five-degree angle or even the table saw in one corner were all targets for the eye. Yet, like a powerful magnet, Sam eventually pulled all her attention back to him.

"Jefferson is supposed to have a pretty good reputation in education and all the liberal arts," Sam remarked, reaching for another cookie.

"He says with a little pride," Sharon teased. "Now who's talking like a proud descendant?"

"I can hardly claim responsibility for the school's reputation," Sam replied with humility. "But I'm glad since my great-great-grandfather was the founder, it's maintained high standards. It would be embarrassing if the school had fallen by the wayside or had no accreditation."

He picked up the pitcher to pour himself another glass of orange juice and held it questioningly toward her. "More?"

"No thanks. We've had—" Dee Dee was no longer sitting quietly beside her. At some point the little girl had slipped out the door without her mother knowing it.

"She left awhile ago. No doubt for more interesting pastures," Sam suggested.

"And so should I," Sharon said, and rose to her feet. "I don't mean more interesting pastures, I mean . . ."

Sam chuckled and raised a quizzical brow as he stood up, purposely close to Sharon. He couldn't help himself from taking an affronted posture and saying, "You mean I've been boring you, too?"

"Nothing could be further from the truth," Sharon blurted, sucking in her breath. Standing this close to him, she could smell the clean, tangy scent of his skin and was on eye level with the exposed wedge of his chest that she'd tried so hard to ignore for the past hour or so. "What I meant was, I need to get back and supervise the boys' work detail."

"You've put those two barbarians to work?"

"How do you know that's what I call them?"

Sam quickly explained, "Dee Dee and I had quite a discussion about men of such ilk. She tells me that's your estimation of people who don't wear jammies." He knew full well what this turn of conversation was doing to her, but he was enjoying the flush rising in her cheeks too much to relent.

She giggled nervously, awareness of Sam's nudity beneath the robe returning all too vividly. "It's a lecture I give often but to no avail." Needing to put some distance between them, she sidestepped, but Sam moved with her.

"Dee Dee says you're an expert on barbarians," he drawled, lifting a finger and twirling it through one of the rich chestnut curls that framed her flushed face.

He was unabashedly putting the move on her, and Sharon couldn't find the strength to stop him. She was trapped between the couch and a pair of velvety gray eyes. She caught her breath when he dropped his hand from her hair and encircled her with his arms. "Sam," she protested weakly.

"According to Dee Dee, I already match your description of a barbarian," Sam said huskily, gently pulling her against him. "So you shouldn't be surprised that I'm about to pillage and plunder," he warned her as he lowered his head.

The touch of his lips was a gentle assault, and the resistance Sharon would have thrown up if he'd been primitively possessive was lost within the melting sensations he aroused in her. He tempted her lips with the tip of his tongue, then settled his mouth over hers.

Sharon lifted her arms, slid her palms along the lapels of his robe to lock her hands behind his neck. Sam gathered her snugly to him as his tongue penetrated beyond her lips, rubbed along her tongue, then moved on to explore every crevice. Sharon's eager response was the bounty he collected for his tender attack.

Her fingertips moved through the dark, waving hair at his nape. Her tongue followed his lead and journeyed into the unknown of his mouth, discovering his taste and finding it to her liking. One of his hands stayed at her waist, his fingers tracing patterns on her smooth skin. He widened his stance as his other hand slid over the gentle arch in the middle of her back, urging her into a more intimate position.

The hard evidence of his unfettered maleness pressed against Sharon's soft abdomen. She was shocked back to her senses from her haze of dreamy lassitude.

Feeling her withdrawal, Sam sensed any persistence on his part to continue would only frighten her. If he came on like Attila the Hun, his first encounter with her would be his last. Reluctantly he loosened his hold and controlled his baser instincts.

Neither Sam nor Sharon was breathing normally when they stepped apart. Withstanding the urge to place her fingertips against her lips to stop their throbbing, she was at a loss for words. She hadn't felt this kind of frustrated desire since she'd been a teenager and she and Mike had jumped to opposite sides of the car when their petting had threatened to rage out of control.

Back then, she had been a virgin and frightened by the heated coil of desire that caused a weakness in her limbs and a moist warmth in her loins. She was almost as frightened by those sensations now. She wasn't dealing with a teenage boy who was as inexperienced as she. She had just been thoroughly and expertly kissed by a man who knew exactly what he was about. And, as a woman, she'd responded, feeling desire for the first time in over three years.

Seeing the confusion and frustration mirrored in her large brown eyes, Sam knew the same emotions were probably reflected in his own. Kissing her had been an unquenchable impulse and his enjoyment of that kiss had been far more than he'd bargained for.

"I suppose I should gallantly say I'm sorry that happened," he began. "But, I'm not. I don't think barbarians apologize anyway."

"No. I don't suppose they do," Sharon agreed, her words slow, slightly breathless. "They don't kiss like that, either."

"You know from experience?"

Sharon searched for an answer as she stepped closer to the door. Experience? She didn't really have any. Mike had been the only man she'd ever kissed. "I didn't claim to be experienced with barbarians, just knowledgeable about their behavior." She smiled unsteadily.

He took a step toward her and challenged, "Are you courageous enough to become more knowledgeable about the behavior of this one?" Before she could respond, he added, "Have dinner with me tomorrow night."

"But I . . . I don't—" she stammered.

"I'm sure you eat, so that's no excuse," he interjected. "I promise to dress respectably." He shoved his hands in his pockets and gave her a crooked grin. "And behave accordingly," he threw in for good measure.

She hedged another moment or two then agreed. She had plenty of built-in baby-sitters for Dee Dee, and it would be good to be in the company of a male of her own generation. It wasn't until she was out of the carriage house and halfway across the yard that she collected her senses. He'd done it again. Sam Jefferson could charm her into anything. She was sure it would be wise to turn right around and cancel the date.

Standing at one of his windows, Sam watched Sharon's progress toward the main house, then saw her slow down and almost stop. *Don't change your mind*, he willed, and almost believed he'd acquired the power of mind-linking when he saw her square her shoulders and continue on her way. Assured that the lady wasn't going to back out, he left his post.

Feeling vitally alive, he decided he might as well get dressed and use his newfound energy constructively. He discarded the idea of donning his work clothes and diving into any of a long list of projects that would bring the carriage house closer to completion. He wasn't that full of energy. He'd check in at his office, instead. He'd been away for two weeks. Even a practice as small and as slow as his must have some work piled up.

At the office he occupied across the main street from the Rhodesboro Bank, Sam discovered a heap of messages on his desk. He quickly sorted them into two piles. One was for Mayor Jefferson, the other for attorney Jefferson. The mayor's stack was much higher than the attorney's but required less concentration. He chose the mayor's, recognizing that his mind wasn't quite as clear as he'd thought.

After a few minutes Sam gave up any pretense of work. Glad that his secretary wasn't there to comment on his daydreaming, he leaned back in his leather-upholstered chair and propped his feet up on his desk. Sharon Markovski occupied the forefront of his thoughts.

He couldn't remember when a woman had felt so good in his arms. Not even Carol, the long-time mistress he'd left behind in Chicago, had fitted so well against his body. His parting from her had been amicable, and in retrospect he could see their relationship had never inspired strong emotion. He'd felt none of the fire that had flared up so quickly between himself and the delectable brown-eyed widow Markovski.

Just as he and his mistress's body had never quite melded, neither had their emotions and thoughts. Carol was the ultimate career woman, fiercely independent and lasciviously liberal. She'd been a beautiful woman on his arm, satisfying in bed and an interesting conversationalist. That's all he'd wanted from her, and that was all she'd offered him.

Sharon was certainly just as intelligent. Her fresh natural beauty was a contrast to Carol's polished sophisticated looks, but no less attractive. Carol was an interesting woman, but Sharon was utterly fascinating. There was something very special about her. Since their bodies were a perfect fit, he wondered it if followed that their emotions and thoughts would blend, as well. If the kiss they'd shared was any indication, taking her to bed would give him more than physical satisfaction.

The direction of his thoughts renewed the desire in his loins. He wanted her more than he'd wanted a woman in years, but questioned the wisdom of becoming involved with a woman like her. She had five children, a factor not easily ignored. He'd steered clear of domestic types...until now. *Hell!* If he had any sense he'd keep on doing so.

3

SHARON'S BEDROOM DOOR opened a crack, and Merry popped her head inside. "He's here." Stepping into the room, she fanned the air with limp wrists. "He is such a *babe!*" she pronounced in adoring awe.

That he is, Sharon almost said, an image of Sam's broad shoulders and lean body draped with nothing but a velvety robe instantly coming to mind. The stomach flutters that had begun more than an hour ago in anticipation of his arrival escalated. For the millionth time she asked herself what she, the mother of five, was doing going out with such a suave, virile man.

She dropped an earring and had to fumble around on the carpet to find it. "Darn, I need at least five more minutes," she muttered frantically. "Oh, why can't I ever get my act together on time?"

"Not to worry, Mom," Merry stated airily. "Mr. Jefferson said for you to take your time, and he apologized for being early."

Glancing at the clock on her nightstand, Sharon confirmed that Sam had indeed arrived a full ten minutes too soon. It might just serve the man right if she took the whole time and left him down in the living room at the mercy of her children. Michael would no doubt challenge him to arm wrestle, while Theresa would trap him into a game of Trivial Pursuit. All the while Dee Dee would be serenading everyone, and over the general din, Tim would be shouting questions about every car Sam had ever owned.

If Merry went downstairs, she might swoon at his feet. And Aunt Di? Sharon didn't think her aunt would resort to any obvious matchmaking. Quickly stepping into her shoes, she gave herself a last once-over in the mirror.

She pulled the tie at the side of her waist a little snugger, thinking the neckline of her wraparound dress might be a bit too low. She wasn't used to wearing such a bright color, but Merry, who'd dragged her to a dress shop that afternoon, had insisted that the deep apricot shade was perfect on her. The silky creation had been a splurge that Sharon could ill afford, and having second thoughts about the wisdom of such an expenditure, she considered taking it off and returning it the next day. She'd saved all the tags just in case.

"You look great," Merry assured, coming to her mother's side. "That color really looks good on you." She placed her arm around Sharon's shoulders. "Everything'll be fine. Go out and have a good time."

Sharon chuckled at the role reversal, then gave her daughter a quick hug. "Thanks, sweetheart. Even old ladies like me get nervous on a first date."

"You're hardly an old lady," Merry admonished. She stepped away, gave her mother a thorough survey and concluded with a wink, "You're one foxy lady tonight, Mom."

Merry scooped up her mother's purse from the bed and handed it to her. "You'd better get down there before Dee Dee convinces him to take her along. She's dressed up in her patent leathers and church dress, you know."

Sharon rolled her eyes heavenward and groaned.

"Don't worry," Merry advised. "I'll go grab the little twirp and lock her in a closet if I have to. You don't need a kid along."

"It probably wouldn't matter if she did come," Sharon supplied resignedly, thinking if Dee Dee was with them, there would be no uncomfortable silence. Her youngest could chatter nonstop for hours. "Mr. Jefferson isn't interested in anything more than a dinner companion. If he were, he certainly wouldn't pick the mother of the hooligans who nearly ran him down yesterday."

Merry sighed disgustedly and shook her head. "Mom . . . you're so naive," she drawled. "The most gorgeous hunk I've ever seen is down there waiting to take you out to dinner, and you're thinking about taking that kid along? You wouldn't be able to do anything."

A flush of warmth spread from Sharon's chest upward as she remembered the feel of Sam's arms around her, the press of his hard body on her softness, the excitement of his kiss. "I'm not planning on *doing* anything."

One hand on the doorknob, Merry suggested slyly, "Without that pest along, you never know…." She was gone before Sharon could respond.

Wondering if that worldly, wise young woman had really been her little girl, Sharon clutched her purse to her chest and left the room. As she descended the stairs, she could hear Theresa playing the piano and knew her eleven-year-old was so immersed in Saint-Saëns's "Le Cygne" that she probably hadn't even noticed Sam's arrival. She gave silent thanks; the Trivial Pursuit box hadn't left the shelf.

A glance through the landing window confirmed that both boys were out on the lawn tossing the football around. So far so good. Only Dee Dee, Merry and Aunt Di were left to cause trouble.

Sharon reached the foyer and headed for the living room. She heard a familiar chirping voice; little Dee Dee's line of conversation indicated very clearly that she was angling for an invitation to dinner. Sam's deep voice wasn't loud enough for Sharon to discern his words.

Then Merry's voice came through. "Come on, kid. You're needed in the kitchen—on the double." And Sharon heard the swish of the swinging kitchen door. So much for Dee Dee.

Only Aunt Di was left to entertain Sam. Sharon crossed her fingers in the hopes that her aunt wasn't beginning to list her niece's attributes. She felt like a Christian about to face the lions as she stepped into the living room.

Upon her entrance, Sam—gentleman that he was—politely rose to his feet. Sharon wanted to seek out the security of the nearest chair to keep from melting into a heap on the floor. She'd seen Sam wilted and perspiring, then seminude. Both times he'd earned a rating close to the mythical perfect ten. However, with him wearing a pearl-toned shirt, slate linen jacket and charcoal pants, his score soared to an incredible fifteen. The garments that covered his body should have softened the hard, lean lines, diminished the effect of that physique on the female libido, but they didn't.

To Sharon, gray had always seemed such a nondescript and lifeless color, but on Sam Jefferson it highlighted the silver at his temples and enhanced the color of his compelling eyes. Somehow, the conservative cut and subdued hues of his clothing emphasized the vitality and excitement that hung like a brilliant aura about the man.

"Hi . . ." Sharon let out breathlessly.

"Good evening," he greeted with the same deep melodic tones that had made her skin tingle the day before. He made a slow, complete turn before her. "Do I pass inspection?"

Totally embarrassed, Sharon stared at him, wide-eyed and mute. Apparently her appraisal of him had been far less than subtle. Somehow she managed, "Inspection?"

"I'm wearing my civilized clothes," Sam supplied, but Sharon still didn't know what he was talking about. Her blank look conveyed her continued confusion and he prompted, "No barbarism tonight; I promise my behavior will match my apparel."

At last Sharon caught his meaning and began to laugh.

Diana Rhodes rose from her chair in the far corner of the room. "I assume that means something, but I can't imagine what," she inserted in passing. "I think I'll get out to the kitchen and see what Merry and Dee Dee are cooking up. It was nice chatting with you, Sam."

"You, too, Diana." Sam offered his arm to a still-smiling Sharon. "Well, pretty lady, I believe we should be going. We have a seven-o'clock reservation at the Colonial House." He tucked Sharon's arm into his and asked, "Trust me not to misbehave?"

Sharon grinned impishly up at him, all her nervousness having fled. "How could I not?" she challenged. "A gentleman would never go back on his promise."

"No, a gentleman wouldn't," he commented silkily.

"And Sam Jefferson is a gentleman," Sharon stated firmly.

"Sam Jefferson has a big mouth," he muttered under his breath, ushering her down the front steps and toward his car.

Sharon shot him a suspicious look. "Excuse me?"

"I, uh, said you've got a great bunch of kids," he improvised, and backed up his statement by waving and smiling at the boys when they called out to him. "I'm glad I got to meet the rest of them tonight."

SOFT LIGHTING and low background music created a relaxing atmosphere in the restaurant. Once a stagecoach inn for weary travelers of the Zane Trail, the Colonial House was still furnished much as it had been in that long-ago era. In deference to twentieth-century fire codes, the sconces along the walls and the huge chandelier in the center of the dining room held flame-shaped bulbs instead of tallow candles. The glowing coals in the huge fireplace at the end of the room were part of a set of artfully designed electric logs, though Sharon was sure she could smell woodsmoke in the air.

She gazed around the gracious old room, reacquainting herself with all the little details that made this such a special place. A waitress, dressed in a long skirt and starched, white apron, whisked past carrying a linen-covered loaf of fragrant bread on a wooden tray. Succumbing to the romance of the historic atmosphere, Sharon found herself mentally clothing her fellow diners in frock coats, long dresses, even fringed buckskins.

"When I was little, Grandma Rhodes, and sometimes Aunt Di, used to bring me here during my visits," Sharon remarked. "I used to pretend I'd walked through a time warp."

"And now?" Sam asked with a maddeningly knowing smile.

Sharon laughed lightly, her large brown eyes glittering with reflected lights from the wall sconce above their table. "Maybe not a time warp, but I'll confess to having rather fanciful thoughts a moment ago."

At Sam's urging, she revealed how with a little imagination, the modern clothing of the other patrons could dissolve into period costumes. With the low lighting and the authentic background setting the scene, she and Sam began a mind game of redressing the diners seated around them.

"See that rather heavyset man at the next table?" she asked, leaning forward and talking very softly so as not to be overheard. "Can't you just picture his collar a little higher, the stiff points jabbing his chin, a silk cravat tied too tightly around his neck? Then, wouldn't he look like a prosperous nineteenth-century banker?"

Squinting his eyes, Sam cast a surreptitious sidelong glance at the neighboring table. "No doubt about it. All he needs is muttonchops and a brocade vest."

"Perfect," Sharon pronounced. "Now, who do you think I see as a rough, woodsman type?"

"Mmm, can't be anyone I know." Knowing very well she was talking about him, he pretended to survey the room. "It's a pretty dignified crowd here tonight. All the barbarians must be in the bar or spruced up so good you can't tell 'em from the gentry. Only civilized folk are allowed in the dining room, you know."

He tugged at his jacket sleeves and brushed imaginary dust from his lapels. "I think I look pretty good, don't you? Took a bath and dressed up in my best bib and tucker."

Sharon laughed at his folksy dialect. "Yes, you did very well. No one would ever know the truth about you."

"You mean I've successfully disguised my primitive tendencies?"

"Absolutely," Sharon confirmed.

"Actually, they're part of my nature," Sam warned with an audacious smile. "But, since I'm in the company of such a beautiful lady, I'm trying my best to suppress them." Then his smile faded and his voice dropped to a deep huskiness. "You really are beautiful, Sharon. You outshine every woman here."

His gaze met hers and locked, telling her more with its velvety intensity than had his words. Sharon felt a thrill of excitement.

"Thank you," she murmured shakily. She felt a flush of warmth in her cheeks. Though she enjoyed his attention, she was also a bit uncomfortable with it. She almost cried out in relief when their waitress arrived with the next course, and Sam's sensual gaze was diverted.

As soon as the waitress had left, Sam lifted his wineglass and offered a toast. "To new friends."

Sharon raised her glass and echoed his words, crossing her fingers that the sentiment would set the stage for the remainder of the evening. She enjoyed being with him, recognized a need to spend time with a man, but any involvement that went beyond friendship was something she wasn't prepared to deal with at this point in her life. She simply didn't have the emotional energy to expend on a torrid affair. The sensual pull between her and Sam had to be withstood, though she doubted she could forget the kiss they'd shared. Nor would she be able to stifle the sensations that warmed her whenever he turned those velvety eyes of his on her.

As he'd done the day before, Sam adroitly steered the conversation to her. Before she knew it, she was telling him about her lifelong thirst for knowledge and how much she had enjoyed the intellectual stimulation of her college classes. She revealed her goals and philosophies more openly with Sam than she'd ever done with anyone. Not her husband nor even Aunt Di had ever listened so intently or seemed so genuinely interested.

"I love to read," Sharon enthused as their coffee was served. "To me, the ability to make sense of and enjoy the written word is a great gift. Without it, people are crippled in spirit, to say nothing of the difficulties they face in getting along in today's world."

"I couldn't agree more." Sam settled his cup into its saucer and smiled warmly. "You're going to make a very fine teacher."

"I'm going to try," she vowed. "I just hope I can land a position as soon as I graduate, preferably somewhere within the county. I don't want to have to uproot the children again, nor do I want to sit around unemployed."

"You shouldn't have much trouble getting a job," Sam assured. "For whatever it's worth, I'll even put in a good word for you with the local school board. I know they don't receive as many applications as they do in the big city schools."

"That would be very kind of you. I really need that job." She let out a long-suffering sigh. "After all, I have five fatherless children to support." With a dramatic flourish, she clasped her hand over her heart.

Her theatrical antics reminded him so much of Dee Dee, Sam couldn't help but laugh. "What's with the poor-pitiful-widow routine?" he asked. "I already promised to put in a good word for you. What more do you want?"

"Just wanted to make sure you did your best," she explained brightly with a carefree laugh.

"Until tonight, I actually wondered where Dee Dee inherited her theatrical ability," Sam admitted, grinning widely.

"Taught the kid everything I know," Sharon confessed.

"I'm doomed. I'm doomed," Sam decreed in mock resignation. "I have a feeling that routine may turn up again and again. I'm sure it's very effective."

With feigned affront, Sharon retorted, "But I am a widow with five children to support."

"Yes you are, but you're anything but helpless."

Their conversation continued in this vein, Sharon savoring every one of the playful gibes he threw at her. For three years people had been pussyfooting around her, feeling so sorry for her that they didn't dare tease her about anything—certainly not her widowed state.

It was such a relief to talk with someone who wasn't afraid she'd burst into tears at any moment. She had even told him how Mike had died and hadn't had to endure the usual uncomfortable albeit well-meaning condolences. When Sam heard that Mike had literally worked himself to death, suffered a fatal heart attack brought on by the oppressive heat in the mill, he had expressed his regret, but hadn't dwelled on it.

She'd mourned Mike's death, and a part of her always would. But she'd long ago accepted that though life might have dealt her a cruel blow, she couldn't cry about it forever. Mike wouldn't have wanted that from her, anyway. Sam was one of the few people she'd met who appeared to understand this.

By the time Sharon and Sam had finished their meal and lingered over several cups of coffee, they had covered a myriad of topics. Sharon finally had had the satisfaction of sitting back and listening to Sam talk about himself. With a few prods from her, he had revealed his reasons for coming back to the small town of his ancestors.

"You made a wise decision," Sharon offered after learning that he'd had not one recurrence of abdominal pain since he'd adopted his new life-style.

Sam dipped his head slightly and said, "Thank you for your confidence, milady. I know I did."

"I get the feeling someone doesn't think so," Sharon ventured. "Your parents, by any chance?"

"My mother. How did you guess?"

Sharon shrugged. "Personal experience."

"You, too, huh?" Sam probed.

"I'm afraid so," Sharon admitted without the reservation she would have felt prior to their evening together. Though she still recognized that she and Sam were worlds apart in experience and sophistication, it looked as though they had much more in common than roots in a small town. "If my parents had their druthers, I'd be living the same life they are. Instead I married my high school sweetheart right after graduation and had five children—we both wanted a big family. Mike made a good life for us, but it wasn't the one my parents would have wanted for me."

"You deviated early," Sam said. "I didn't rebel until my health was threatened. You'd think my mother would approve of this move since my father worked himself to death like your husband did. Dad had a heart attack, too."

"In defense of your mother," Sharon inserted, "sometimes it's a little difficult for parents to sit back and let children lead their own lives, no matter how old they are. So many years have been spent guiding and protecting them, that it's hard to know when to stop."

"I have the feeling you're talking about yourself as a parent," Sam put forth with the understanding Sharon had come to expect.

Sharon chose not to respond immediately, taking a breather to analyze just how she felt about Sam's ability to read her so well after such a short time. Maybe they were on the same wavelength, kindred spirits, Aunt Di would probably say. Looking at Sam, she realized he was exactly the type of man her parents would have wanted her to marry. That thought should have made her uncomfortable and wary, but strangely, it did not.

"It's not easy letting children grow up," she began finally. "When they're babies, you have to believe you know what's best for them or you'd drive yourself crazy with insecurity. As I said, parents have a difficult time learning when to turn the responsibility over to the kid. After all, for years he couldn't even tie his shoelaces by himself."

"From what I've seen, you're managing quite well," he complimented. "Your kids seem to be pretty well adjusted."

"You've only been around my mob for a day," she reminded him with a self-depreciating grin. "I am by no means an all-knowing, perfect mother with a smoothly running household. I try to keep hold of the reins, but they're all pulling away in five different directions. Sometimes I end up screaming my head off to remind them who's in charge."

"You, with eyes as soft and warm as a doe's, actually raise your voice?" he teased.

"What a short memory you have, sir."

"Not short, just selective," he returned quickly with a smile that warmed Sharon to her toes.

Struggling to control her clamoring senses, Sharon turned the conversation back toward Sam. Her curiosity about the extensive renovations in progress at his carriage house prompted her to ask about them. Sam went on at some length about his projections for his house, surprising Sharon completely with the revelation that he was doing most of the work himself.

"It's good therapy after spending a day using nothing but your brain," he explained after he'd regaled her with tales of his first attempts at carpentry. Finally, realizing they were the only remaining patrons in the dining room, Sam suggested they be kind to the Colonial House staff and let them close up the place.

"You're a fascinating woman, Sharon," Sam said as he escorted her out of the restaurant, and he'd never meant a compliment more sincerely. She was lovely, inside and out; so fresh and honest he felt positively renewed around her.

"And you're an intriguing man, Sam," Sharon returned. "There can't be many who would listen to a woman babble on about herself for an entire evening without complaining."

"I enjoyed it," Sam maintained. He opened the car door for her. "I could hardly accuse you of dominating the conversation, when I spent a good deal of time discussing the intricacies of wood-panel installation." He winked as she stepped past him and lowered herself into the car.

"I enjoyed it," she mimicked, then smiled up at him and proclaimed, "You're a true gentleman, Sam Jefferson."

"I told you, I keep my promises." He closed the passenger door and silently cursed his misplaced sense of honor as he walked to the other side of the car. Sharon's smile had drawn his gaze to her lips, and he was suddenly reminded of how delicious she'd tasted, how good she felt in his arms.

Sam started the car and pulled away from the curb, purposely keeping his speed way below the limit. He didn't want the evening to end. With someone else, he probably would have suggested a nightcap at her home or his, knowing where it would lead.

However, he knew that if he attempted to bring about such an end to the evening with Sharon, he'd not only be betraying her trust, but he'd be the lowest creep in the world. No matter how many fireworks their kiss had set off, Sharon wasn't ready for more. And for reasons he couldn't define, he knew he didn't want a one-night stand with her. Somehow, he was sure that was all he'd have if they slept together tonight.

As he turned the car into their street, he was still unsure how he was going to proceed. He felt like a kid on his first date. *Should I kiss her or shouldn't I?*

What'll I do if he invites me in? Sharon wondered nervously as they drove up the driveway. Then she began to question whether or not she should invite *him* in. If she was a sophisticated, worldly woman she'd know what to do. But she wasn't; she was Sharon Markovski.

She'd never been in this kind of situation before, and she'd never made love with anyone but her husband. Considering the way she'd melted into Sam's arms the previous afternoon, Sharon knew with certainty that she'd fall into Sam's bed very easily and willingly if he coaxed her. Oh, she wanted him, but the question remained as to whether she was ready for that kind of intimacy. No, she decided. But the idea was still tempting.

Sam turned into the driveway. A quick glance at the main house told Sharon that at least her older children were still up; the lights in the den were on. That meant they were watching late-night television. It also meant that unless the kids were totally oblivious to anything but the images on the television screen, they'd know that she and Sam had just pulled into the driveway. She'd have to go into the house straightaway or be subjected to questions she might not want to answer.

"Mind if I pull ahead and park in my garage?"

"Of course not," Sharon replied at once. No matter what the kids might ask, she wasn't ready for the evening to end. The walk from his garage to the house would prolong it for a few minutes. She wondered if Sam had had the same thought.

Inside the garage, Sam turned off the engine and got out of the car. As he rounded the rear and started toward the passenger side, he was still uncertain of his next action. When he opened the door, the interior light illuminated Sharon's face. Her expression matched the nervousness he felt.

He knew what he had to do, or more to the point couldn't do, but he almost lost his resolve when her breasts brushed his arm as he helped her out of the car. He let go of her hand immediately and put a little distance between them as they walked out of the garage. It was far safer not to touch her at all, just breathing in the sweet scent of her was causing him trouble.

He'd promised to be civilized, and he feared if he so much as touched her he'd end up dragging her behind the nearest bush. He tried to keep his vow in mind despite the roaring need aching in his loins. They were friends, just friends . . . buddies . . . at least for now.

"It's a pretty night, isn't it?" Sharon stated more than asked.

"Yes, it is. Plenty of bright stars up there."

"Mmm." Sharon breathed deeply, pulling in the fragrance of the night, a mixture of dampness, the faint perfume of flowers and the scent of the newly mowed grass. Yet something wasn't quite right. Of course she was relieved that he hadn't asked her to finish off the evening at his house. But he could have at least held her hand. Or put his arm around her as he walked her the short distance to her back porch, for heaven's sake. "I love summer evenings, don't you?"

"Yes, it's cooler and more peaceful."

"You value your peace, don't you, Sam?" Sharon asked pointedly, and mounted the first of the porch steps.

"I suppose so," he answered carefully, wondering what she was leading up to.

Sharon turned quickly. One step above him, she was almost Sam's height, her face very close to his. "We Markovskis have disrupted that peace, haven't we?"

"Have I complained?" His eyebrows drew together in a frown. Her children, she, had disrupted his peace, but not in the way she meant.

"No, but I'm sure we have, and I'm sorry." Abruptly she reached up and smoothed the furrows between his brows. "And now I'm sorry I made you frown at me."

"I'm not frowning at you, but this paranoia you have about noise." He caught her hand and pressed a kiss into her palm before bringing it down to her side. It fit too well in his to let it go. Not yet, not until he'd kissed her. Just a little kiss, a kiss between friends, he rationalized. He'd spend another frustrating night after tasting that soft sweet mouth of hers, but he'd be even more frustrated if he didn't at least kiss her good-night.

"I'm no expert, but aren't kids supposed to make some noise?" he asked.

Sharon nodded. The light hold of his large, warm hand upon hers sent pleasant tingles up her arm and through her body. The way he was looking at her with those incredibly warm eyes increased the pleasure; she wanted to sigh at the exquisite tenderness she saw there. So caught up was she in the husky tone of his voice and the softness of his gaze that she barely registered his words.

"If you keep apologizing, I'm going to think I do have something to complain about. And so far, my friend, I have no complaints," he said as he lowered his head toward hers.

Sam searched her eyes for any sign of rejection. Finding none, he raised his free hand and curved his palm lightly to her cheek. "Never apologize before the crime," he advised.

"Is that some free legal advice?" she asked breathlessly, swaying involuntarily toward him.

"Not exactly free," he said, then brushed his lips across hers very lightly in an achingly sweet kiss.

4

"OH MAN." Tim gazed with wide-eyed awe at Sam's 1974 Jensen Healy sports car. "That is one bad lookin' machine." He ran his hands lovingly over the gleaming front fender. His expression, however, became suddenly pained when he encountered a large dent and blistering rust around the cornering lamp.

Sam folded the canvas tarp he'd pulled from the vehicle and tossed it out of the way. "The power plant's in pretty fair condition, but the chassis needs a lot of work."

Slowly rounding the low-slung black convertible, Tim was obviously cataloging each scrape, dent and fleck of rust. "What kind of guts does she have?"

"She's got a Lotus engine and does zero to sixty in 9.7 seconds." Sam couldn't help boasting, though he now appreciated the car more for its classic lines and expert engineering than its capacity for speed.

Watching Tim study every inch of the Jensen, Sam wondered if his own expression had been as worshipful when he'd first seen the car. Possibly, he decided, remembering how excited he'd been five years ago when he'd saved it from deterioration in an isolated garage. Though he'd not yet started on its restoration, he had kept it from going any further downhill.

"How much needs to be done to the engine?" Tim inquired. He reached for the hood release, but waited until Sam gave him an approving nod. Eagerly he flung open the hood and peered with even wider eyes at the double overhead camshaft and fuel-injected engine.

"It'll start, but she runs pretty rough. Among other things, the exhaust system needs work." Sam ambled over to stand alongside of Tim and peer at the engine.

He remembered himself at about Tim's age, when he and his father had undertaken the restoration of a vintage Cadillac. That yellow, heavily-chromed, 1939 convertible had become the ultimate "cruise-mobile." Sam had enjoyed working on that car with his dad almost as much as he'd enjoyed eventually driving it. It was with a stab of sorrow that he recalled his father had lived only long enough to see the car finished and had driven it only once.

Sam stood with the slight, dark-haired youth in a long moment of silent harmony and appreciation for the mechanical wonder under the hood. Guessing at what was going on in Tim's mind, Sam fished in his pocket and handed over a set of keys. "Go ahead, start her up. I uncovered her so I could turn over the engine a few times."

"Gee thanks," Tim enthused, his brown eyes full of barely suppressed excitement.

A LOUD EXPLOSION, then a window-shaking roar shattered the serenity of the early evening. Sharon nearly dropped the pan she was sliding from the oven. "Good Lord!" she exclaimed.

Merry and Theresa, who had been in the midst of setting the table, clapped their hands over their ears. "What's going on?"

The thunderous noise continued, and Sharon ran to the kitchen window, sure that at least a thousand motorcyclists had convened in the backyard. Rather than a swarm of Hell's Angels, she saw a thick, blue cloud of smoke pouring from Sam's garage.

The swinging door banged open as Michael shot through the kitchen and raced out the back door saying, "You hear that power plant?"

Sharon, not having a clue what he was talking about, called out for him to stop, but he didn't heed her warning. She raced after him, heart pounding. As she descended the back-porch steps, she saw Michael's blond head and broad shoulders disappear into a cloud of exhaust. Fearing her son's imminent asphyxiation, she waved her arms at the fumes and charged in after him.

Inside, the air was fairly clear and the fumes not as overpowering as Sharon had imagined. The source of the deafening racket was the meanest-looking black car she'd ever seen, and her second-born son was the zealot whose lead foot was on the accelerator. Michael stood beside the beastly vehicle with a jealous gleam in his eyes. And leaning against a support pole was Sam, wearing the same glazed look of rapture as Tim.

Hands over her ears, Sharon tried shouting, but her voice was a frail opponent pitted against the roaring engine. She had to tug on Sam's shirt sleeve just to get his attention. Seeing her distress, he signaled Tim to switch off the ignition.

After one more explosive backfire, there was silence. Blessed silence. Sharon savored it for a second or two before asking, "What is that? A jet engine?"

"Close," Sam acknowledged. Grinning, he inquired, "Little too loud for you?"

"That's an understatement," Sharon said through a cough. "I'm surprised any of you can still breathe, let alone hear."

"Huh?" a trio of varying-leveled voices responded, then all of them had the audacity to cast her identical condescending machismo grins. It was as if suddenly they'd joined forces against the poor, ignorant female who couldn't possibly comprehend the joy of having one's eardrums split by the roar of a monster car's engine.

They were right. Sharon couldn't understand the male fascination with cars. The glare she turned on all of them told at least her sons exactly what she thought.

"Okay, now that you boys have finished shaking up the neighborhood, it's time for dinner," she stated, including Sam in the condemnation. She started to leave the garage and then stopped. Dropping her stern expression, she smiled. "Sam? We'd enjoy having you if you'd like to have dinner with us."

To sweeten the invitation, Michael threw in, "Stuffed pork chops tonight, and Mom's are the best. She baked a cherry pie, too."

"She's a real good cook," Tim chimed in.

Sam turned the full force of his vote-winning smile on her. "Oh she is, is she? Good food and a gorgeous hostess," he said, unable to keep his eyes from drifting to the fullness of her breasts, which pressed against her periwinkle blouse, then down over the gentle curves revealed by her white shorts. "Sounds like an invitation too good to pass up."

Sharon wanted to crawl beneath the cobblestone floor of the garage. Her sons' comments had been enough to bring a blush to her cheeks, and Sam's enveloping gaze had brought a flush of warmth to her entire body. For days those marvelous eyes of his had looked at her with nothing but friendliness. Now, he was looking at her as if he expected to have her for dinner. She could only hope that the boys were so enthralled with the classic car that they hadn't noticed their mother was about to join the grease spots on the garage floor.

Involuntarily her eyes went to Sam's mouth. Lord! Her body was fast becoming a hot quivering mass, as she imagined how those sensual lips would feel against her bare skin. "I...I'll go have Merry set another plate." She backed toward the garage door. "Hustle up, you guys, or those pork chops will be cold. I've already taken them out of the oven."

On the way to the house, she got her pulse under control, and managed a fairly good job of convincing herself that she could have imagined that devouring look in Sam's eyes. It had probably been nothing more than her own vanity. She'd wanted him to look at her with as much desire as her quickened breathing and rapt expression had doubtless revealed to him.

She directed Merry to arrange another place at the table and ignored the swooning look in her daughter's eyes when she learned the identity of their guest. Busying herself at the counter, Sharon worried about the wisdom of subjecting Sam to a family dinner.

Eating with five kids was going to be nothing like the quiet, relaxing meal she'd shared with Sam three nights before. The poor man was risking a flare-up of ulcers. As a bachelor, he was used to peace and tranquility, conditions almost never present during a meal in her household.

It wasn't that her children had no table manners. It was just that the evening meal had traditionally been the time when everyone talked about everything and anything that had happened to them during the day. She supposed she should be grateful that her teenagers hadn't turned moody and hostile on her. Unlike many of their peers, they still openly discussed their activities with her. But five kids were five kids, and that meant noise and confusion.

Still, she couldn't very well not have extended Sam the invitation when he'd been standing right there with the boys. Pouring lemon butter over the broccoli spears, she reasoned that it had been the neighborly thing to do. No more. No less.

Of course, there hadn't been any opportunity for anything else. Besides, she didn't want anything but friendship. Of course she didn't. The last thing she needed was a flaming affair. A friend was a precious treasure. Just because that friend happened to be the most exciting and best-looking man she'd ever seen shouldn't make one iota of difference.

"Sam's going to let us help fix up his car," Tim called out, heralding the entrance of the three macho mechanics. He raced past her to wash his greasy hands in the small lavatory off the kitchen. Michael lumbered in, deep in a conversation with Sam that continued as they followed Tim's lead and washed up.

Sharon picked up some gibberish about rpm's, in-lines, cc's, and cylinders. She knew better than to hope that Michael's scientific-sounding discussion would transfer over into his schoolwork. Though geometric theorems had never found a secure niche in Michael's memory banks, he displayed a photographic memory for the workings of the internal combustion engine and the countless statistics found in *Road and Track*.

Sharon had no expertise when it came to cars. Only a strong belief in the equality of women kept her from throwing mechanics into an imaginary box labeled "for males only." She'd been quietly relieved that her boys could discuss these things with each other and hadn't challenged her with their knowledge. Still, she felt a little left out listening to her sons pump Sam for all he knew on the subject of car engines.

Since Aunt Di had gone to a benefit dinner, Merry had logically set Sam's plate and silverware at Aunt Di's customary place at the far end of the table. It wasn't until Sharon raised her head after the blessing and looked down the long length of the harvest table that she realized the implied significance of the placement. To an outsider, they would have appeared the epitome of a happy family, sitting down to their evening meal. Mommy at one end, the boys on one side, the girls on the other, and Daddy seated at the head of the table. She crossed her fingers and hoped that Sam wasn't thinking the same thing.

He certainly seemed to be enjoying himself, so Sharon relaxed a little. He expounded upon the intricacies of that supersonic jet engine out in his garage for a while longer and then moved on to sports, specifically the Cincinnati Reds' chances for the pennant.

Without a father, uncles or a nearby grandfather, the boys were obviously desperate for a man's company. Michael and Tim were enthralled. However, the Markovski males weren't the only members of the family to display an almost worshipful admiration for Sam. The girls, though Sharon suspected they didn't understand what was being said any more than she did, seemed to hang on Sam's every word.

Sharon knew what was behind Merry's fascination. The adolescent blonde, teetering on the edge of womanhood, had made no secret of how good-looking she thought Sam was. As for Theresa and Dee Dee's avid attention, Sharon prayed it was inspired by good manners, not their hope that said man might become a permanent part of their gathering.

The boys hadn't said much about her date with Sam, but the girls had. Merry and Theresa had made it very clear that they thought their mother was slightly crazed in her insistence that she and Sam would stay merely friends.

Dee Dee, having never really known her father, had bluntly asked if Sam was going to fill that position. The little redhead wasn't pleased with her mother's negative answer, and Sharon wouldn't put it past her to come right out and ask Sam if he was contemplating the instant fatherhood of five. Seated right next to her, though, Sharon was ready to place a muzzling hand over the child's mouth, if necessary.

Sam forced a break in the sports-dominated conversation to compliment the cook. "These are delicious," he commented, indicating the cornbread-stuffed pork chops. "The best I've ever had."

"Told you," Michael remarked, stretching a long powerful arm toward the center of the table and scooping another chop—his fourth—from the platter. A mountain of parsleyed new potatoes—his third gigantic helping—followed the chop.

Sharon accepted Sam's compliment, then pressed her lips together and dipped her head to hide her smirk at his astounded expression. Most people were prepared for the amount of food a teenage boy could put away in one sitting. However, Michael's hearty consumption far surpassed the norm. Sharon had to admire the way Sam effected a quick recovery and managed to keep his chin from dropping too far as Michael nearly inhaled his extra portions.

As if on cue, the phone then started ringing. Though Theresa had phone duty and told each caller that supper was in progress and their calls would be returned, the intermittent jangling served as a catalyst, increasing the number and volume of discussions at the table. By meal's end, when every crumb of the ten-inch pie had been consumed and the children had dashed off, Sam looked like a victim of shell shock.

"Sometimes the din is a bit much for the uninitiated," Sharon offered, settling back in her chair to enjoy the momentary peace that prevailed in the kitchen. "I imagine you'll think twice before coming to dinner again."

"There you go, warning me about the imagined horrors of associating with your children," Sam chided. His gray eyes, so strangely warm for their color, focused directly on her, and Sharon was reminded of all the tenderness they'd conveyed when he'd kissed her. It was a gaze far different than the lusty one he'd settled on her out in the garage, and she didn't know how to interpret it. She couldn't figure out what he wanted from her. He behaved as if he wanted them to be no more than friends, yet his expression often said otherwise.

"I still maintain that they're a great group," Sam went on, seemingly unaware of Sharon's confusion. "I'll admit being a bit taken aback a time or two during the meal, but your good cooking more than made up for the confusion."

"Thank you, kind sir...I think," Sharon responded, deciding to concentrate on the platonic side of their relationship and ignore all his other signals.

Reaching for the plates around her, she stacked them together. Rising, she started to carry them toward the sink. She heard a clatter of plates behind her and turned back to see Sam following her lead. "Please, you don't have to do that," she protested.

"It's the least I can do to repay you for that meal," he insisted, balancing a tower of plates on one hand and a stack of empty serving bowls in the other.

Sharon held her breath as he passed by, fearing that any minute Aunt Di's china would slither from his hand and crash to the floor. As soon as his burdens were safely on the counter, she asked, "Where did you learn to do that?"

"In college," he told her as he returned to the table and gathered up the silverware. "I belonged to a very democratic fraternity. Everyone had to take their turn at busing tables."

He started filling the sink with water, but Sharon stopped him. "We run a democratic household here, too. It's Tim and Merry's job to wash the dishes tonight. My assignment was to cook and clear."

"I like the way you run your household, lady," Sam stated, his "toothpaste ad" smile at its most sparkling. "I really hate washing dishes."

"So do I," Sharon confessed, returning Sam s infectious grin. "As soon as I round up the kitchen crew, I'm getting out of here for a little while. I start a summer seminar next week, and this may be one of the last free evenings I have."

Sam joined Sharon in her escape, which turned out to be a walk though the woods behind the house. As they approached the grove, he quizzed her about the upcoming seminar and her reasons for taking it. She started by explaining the course content, panel discussions of elementary-school teaching methods and educational philosophies, then moved on to her reasons for signing up. "It's a noncredit course, and I thought it would help me ease back into the academic world," Sharon told him as they entered the edge of the forest. "It's been a while since I've really had to study, and I'm a little worried about adjusting." Her new, understanding friend, Sam, was by her side, and she felt free to reveal her plans, even some of her insecurities to him.

"I can imagine how you feel. I'm not so sure I'd find going back to school very easy. Taking notes and studying for exams is a science in itself, and I expect I'd be a little rusty," Sam admitted.

The quiet of the small forest worked its magic, and as Sharon and Sam strolled down one of the paths, speaking little, they let the beauty around them dominate their thoughts. For Sharon, it was the first opportunity she'd had to reacquaint herself with the interesting rock formations and gnarled old trees she hadn't seen since she'd been about ten.

A bird sang out from high in a tree they passed under, and its mate answered from deeper in the woods. A field mouse scurried across the path and disappeared beneath the fallen leaves beyond. The sound of a woodpecker tapping in search of his dinner provided a staccato background for the soft cooing of a pair of doves. Hearing the blend of sounds, Sharon was intrigued by the knowledge that the forest, small as it was, was home to so many varieties of life, all living in harmony and balance. In a hushed voice, she revealed that thought to Sam.

"I find a walk in these woods helps put things into perspective," he agreed. "At first it seems so quiet and then when you listen and observe carefully, you realize how much activity is going on here. It reminds me that we're all integral parts of the universe, and we humans shouldn't put ourselves above it all."

"We sound like a pair of naturalists," Sharon returned lightly.

"We do, don't we?" Sam smiled down at her, then stopped and patted the smooth top of a large boulder. "Want to sit awhile?"

"That's my thinking rock!" Sharon exclaimed with joy at being reunited with an old friend. The only such huge boulder in the immediate area, it was located beside the creek. She scrambled to the top of the rock, using the indentations along the side for footing.

"When I was a little girl, I'd pretend that the spirits of the forest had placed this rock here just for me. It had magical qualities. I worked out a lot of problems sitting here." She reclined, propped herself on her elbows and closed her eyes. The last glowing rays of the setting sun wreathed her head and brought out the deep auburn highlights in her chestnut curls.

Sam was free to study her unnoticed. Her face was so guileless and so very pretty. There was beautiful, and glamorous, and there was pretty—a special, natural beauty that very few women could claim. Sharon Markovski was pretty.

She also had a fully-curved figure that made him ache with the need to possess her. He doubted she had any idea of what a seductive picture she made. Sam was sure she didn't realize that with each breath her breasts strained against her blouse. That her smooth legs beneath her shorts beckoned his hands to start at her trim ankles and skim all the way up to her silky thighs.

He wanted her all right. What man wouldn't? She was Lorelei, sunning herself on a rock, enticingly beautiful. But like the legendary Lorelei, she could lure him to destruction. Destruction, certainly, to the kind of life he enjoyed and intended to keep on enjoying.

He reminded himself again that she had five children, was very much family oriented and that any intimacy with her would be expected to lead to a serious involvement. Marriage. Everything about her spelled that word. Sam respected the institution but had no desire to enter it himself. He enjoyed his freedom, his solitude and the peaceful life he'd settled into.

Leaning against a tree, he folded his arms across his chest and cleared his throat. "Do you still think some woodland deity set the rock here?"

Sharon pushed herself up, moving out of the golden ray of sun. She opened her eyes, and the spell was broken. Sam was relieved. Lorelei's promised pleasures were beginning to seem worth the cost. Laughing self-consciously, Sharon responded to his question. "Not after I learned about the great glaciers and how they pushed rocks from Canada this far south. I liked my own explanation better, but I came to accept that my rock wasn't put here by magic. Knowledge makes you face up to reality."

"And reality is something we all must face," Sam stated humorlessly.

"Reality isn't all that bad," Sharon returned merrily, missing the grim set of Sam's face as she scooted down from the rock.

"Sometimes it can be."

Startled by the bleak tone in Sam's voice, Sharon lost her footing. The heels of her sandals slithered past the indentations and she pitched forward. In the nick of time, Sam stepped in front of her and kept her from landing amidst the rushes growing along the muddy bank of the creek.

Sharon's hands automatically clutched at Sam's shoulders when she fell against him. Just as automatically, Sam's arms went around her. He held her close and Sharon melted against him, welcoming the solidity of his body after the panicky feeling of flying into space.

The harsh intake of his breath brought her face up. She hadn't thought she'd slammed into him hard enough to hurt him, but he looked as if he'd been wounded. "Thanks for saving me. I'm sorry if I—"

"I'm the one who's sorry," he interrupted, then abruptly set her away from him. Before she could question his enigmatic statement, he held out his hand to her. "Come on, I think we'd better head out of these woods before it gets dark and we lose our way."

Sharon placed her hand in his, smiling up at him as his warm fingers closed over hers. Her smile was met with a pained look. "Sam?"

He stared into her big brown eyes for a long moment, then swore, "Oh hell. I'm damned if I do and I'm damned if I don't." With a groan of surrender, he pulled her against him.

His mouth brushed her softly, and when he heard her fluttering little cry of surprise it shattered what was left of his control. "Let me have your mouth . . . please," he pleaded, and took the wild beating of her heart as his answer.

Sharon didn't move; she couldn't. No matter what she'd told herself, she was as desperate for this moment as he was. Her heart's pounding blended with his as he cradled her in the curve of his hips. She could feel the hot threat of his body against her and knew no fear. His mouth was tender as his lips taught her new sensations, unique responses to his touch.

She accepted the wild, demanding thrust of his tongue and met it with equal passion. It had been so long since she'd felt this way—alive, burning, blazing with need. Her breasts flattened against his chest and her fingers splayed over his spine. Sharon clung to him, arching her body toward him. She was blind and deaf to the warnings of her conscience when every instinct told her to give in to the glory in his kiss, the urgency of his touch, the passion in his strong, rigid body. She moved sensuously, like a flame upon him.

Sam broke the weld on a tortured breath. His eyes blazed silver, wearing into her. "No more," he choked out gruffly. "One more minute of this, and I'll take you on the forest floor."

Trembling with frustration, Sharon fought for control. "I'm sorry."

"I'm not, but to tell you the truth, lady, you scare the hell out of me," Sam confessed as he gulped air.

Sharon stared at him, openmouthed, feeling as if the wind had just been knocked out of her. "Why?" she questioned, nonplussed.

"I've always stayed away from hearth and home-type women," he admitted. "The thought of love, marriage and a baby carriage has never appealed to me."

Sharon had heard similar declarations before but this time, from this man, she felt an overwhelming disappointment. "I . . . I understand," she murmured haltingly. "I come with lots of strings attached."

Sam saw the hurt on her face and felt like a first-class louse. He wanted her badly, but wasn't ready to take on all those strings she'd referred to. He tried to be as honest as he could, give her fair warning. "I like your kids, Sharon, and I like you. Whenever I touch you all I can think about is taking you to bed. But I don't think it's a good idea for us to get involved. You couldn't handle an affair, and I couldn't handle being part of your family. I'm thirty-eight years old and pretty much of a loner. I'm happy that way."

Sharon bent her head to hide her humiliation. "That's honest. Thanks for telling me before I made a bigger fool out of myself."

"I'm the fool," he contradicted her.

After a long pause he held out his hand as he'd done moments before, this time far more tentatively. "Can we still be friends?"

Covering her true feelings, Sharon agreed. "Sure."

Responding to the gentle pleading and soft regret in his eyes, Sharon placed her hand in his open palm. Swinging their clasped hands between them, Sam guided Sharon along the path leading out of the woods.

5

UNMINDFUL OF THE DAMAGE the rough granite was doing to the smooth leather of his loafers, Sam dug his heels into the rough depressions in the side of the boulder. He propped one elbow on a bent knee and supported his chin with his fist. He'd been sitting on this rock in one position or another for at least an hour, and he was no better off than he'd been when he'd first climbed up on the blasted thing. It was no good. Sharon's "thinking rock" wasn't helping his thinking one bit.

Believing the rock might help him achieve some semblance of peace for even one minute, let alone sixty of them, he mused, was testimony to his extreme state of desperation. The only conclusion he'd reached while perched here was that the peaceful life he'd enjoyed for three years had come to an abrupt end.

Five children had moved in next door. Good kids. Nice kids. Kids he was growing to like a great deal. Not a day went by that he didn't have some sort of contact with one of them. The simple life he'd been leading wasn't so simple anymore. But those children weren't half the cause of his life being turned upside down.

Their delectable mother was driving him absolutely crazy. He'd seen her for brief minutes of friendly con-

if you liked <u>this</u> story
...try our Preview Service

Get 4 FREE full-length Harlequin Temptation® books

Plus

this eye-catching, storeall cosmetic bag

Plus a surprise free gift

Plus lots more!

Our Preview Service is just that...it entitles you to "sneak previews" of the newest four Harlequin Temptation novels every month—months before they are in stores—at 11%-OFF retail on any books you keep (just $1.99 each)—with Free Home Delivery in the bargain.

Moreover, you can quit any time. You don't even have to accept a single selection, and the gifts are yours to keep no matter what—our thanks to you for loving romance as much as we. A super sweet deal if ever there was one!

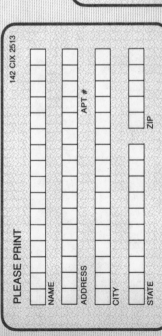
Harlequin Temptation Free Gifts–Free Prizes

38786

WIN A GREAT PRIZE

YES I'll try the Harlequin Preview Service under the terms specified herein. Send me 4 free books and all the other FREE GIFTS. I understand that I also automatically qualify for ALL "Super Celebration" prizes and prize features advertised in 1986. I have written my birthday below. Tell me on my birthday what I win.

▲ If you are NOT signing up for Preview Service, DO NOT use seal. You can win anyway. ▲

FILL IN BIRTHDAY INFORMATION BELOW

MONTH | DATE

this month's featured prize—a dozen roses + 12 $100 bills on winner's birthday + as an added bonus lovely 14k birthstone earrings for 101 monthly winners.

PLEASE PRINT

142 CIX 2513

NAME

ADDRESS   APT #

CITY

STATE   ZIP

Gift offer limited to new subscribers, one per household, and terms and prices subject to change.

Harlequin
"Super Celebration" Sweepstakes

901 Fuhrmann Blvd.
P.O. Box 1867
Buffalo, NY 14240-1867

PLACE
1ST CLASS
STAMP
HERE

versation every day since that evening when he'd declared her off-limits to himself. Where had that moment of insane nobility gotten him? Nowhere. He couldn't ignore the desire he felt for her any longer. It was too strong.

Sam cursed himself for ever having vowed to be a gentleman around her. That crazy promise had been a seemingly harmless quip at the time, a bit of business to tease her into going out with him. Now, however, he felt as though he'd been hoisted on his own petard, as they said.

Sharon had probably forgotten the vow but he couldn't. Considering his damnable lofty principles, the kind of woman Sharon was and how he felt about taking on her children, having anything but a platonic relationship with her was out.

A *gentleman* didn't go back on his word. A *gentleman*, who intended to keep his bachelor status, didn't initiate an intimate relationship with a woman when he knew right from the start that said woman wasn't in the market for a casual affair.

The crunch of a foot on dried leaves followed by a soft giggle brought Sam out of his contemplation. He turned toward the sound and called out, "Theresa?"

A smaller, younger version of the subject of Sam's tormenting thoughts stepped shyly from behind a bush at the edge of the clearing. "Hi," she offered tentatively. "How did you know it was me?"

Sam smiled. Straightening his legs, he slid down from the rock. "Your giggle gave you away," he told her. He glanced at his watch and shrugged. "Besides, I run into you out here almost every day about this time. Supper over?"

Theresa nodded. "Did I disturb you?"

"Nope. I was just sitting here wishing someone would help me identify that bird—" Sam touched Theresa's shoulder and pointed toward a tiny red-throated bird fluttering near a trumpet vine. "Right over there," he finished in a whisper.

"It's a ruby-throated hummingbird," she whispered.

Together they watched the tiny bird take the nectar from the orange blossoms along the vine twining up a tree trunk. Not until the bird had drunk its fill, did either of them utter a sound. When it had flitted off and disappeared into the forest, Theresa turned to Sam with light accusation in her eyes. "You knew that was a hummingbird."

"Yeah. I was hoping I'd trip you up. Do you know the scientific name?"

"*Archilochus colubris!*" Theresa supplied pridefully.

"Darn! You've been studying. I thought I'd trip you up for once." He and Theresa had discovered they had a mutual interest in bird-watching and had begun a playful challenging game of identification of the many species to be found in Appleton Woods.

"You did yesterday," she quickly reminded.

"Ah yes, that wood thrush, you thought was a young robin," Sam said with exaggerated satisfaction. "Did that make us even?" He grinned when Theresa pulled out her ever-present spiral pad and identification book.

Tongue in cheek, he tried for complete sobriety as the scholarly young girl riffled through the pages. A truly serious birder, Theresa kept an accurate record of every species she identified. She not only listed the names, both common and scientific, but sketched a drawing beside each entry. On one page, she kept a running tally of their respective spottings.

She frowned, having finished counting the little marks in their separate columns. "You're ahead by two."

"I'll keep my mouth shut on the next two I see, if you tell me what you were laughing about when you first arrived," Sam bargained. Theresa's features clouded slightly, and she looked decidedly uncomfortable. "Please, Theresa," he coaxed.

"Well..." she hedged, a rosy blush flooding her face. "You." She looked down at the toes of her tennis shoes. "You looked like a picture of a statue in one of Aunt Di's books."

Sam sent her a puzzled look and she elaborated. "It's a man sitting on a rock."

Sam chuckled, immediately identifying the sculpture Theresa was describing and seeing himself in the pose. "Rodin's *The Thinker*. So, you know about great works of art as well as great works of music, Theresa," he stated, more than asked. "You're a Renaissance scholar, my bird-watching, piano-playing, historian friend."

Her answering smile was a beam of sunny radiance. Sam felt pleased, and rewarded.

As Sam and Theresa trooped through brush, searching for the elusive hummingbird's nest, he realized how much he enjoyed these times with her—and the reason why. The way she tilted her head, the softness of her eyes, reminded him of her mother, as did the color of her hair, the shape of her face, even her bone structure.

The thought struck him that it would be intriguing to watch Theresa grow up. It was impossible to have affection for Sharon without feeling something toward her children; they were so much a part of her. Being privy to these years with Theresa would be almost like having had them with her mother. Odd that with other women he'd had no interest or curiosity about their childhoods, yet he wanted to know everything about Sharon, and her children often divulged things about her that made him feel he'd known her all her life.

After parting from Theresa and returning to the carriage house, Sam was treated to his daily serenade from Dee Dee. Sometime after he'd applauded enthusiastically and sent the little soloist on her way with another dime in her pocket, the eldest Markovski daughter appeared at his door.

"Hi," Merry greeted in a breathless rush.

"Hello, Merry, what can I do for you?" Sam asked, smiling warmly. Merry said nothing, simply stared up at him, her face growing more pink with each passing second. "Merry?" He tried gently to pull some speech out of her. She seemed to be in a trance. He resisted the temptation to snap his fingers before her face.

Finally she blinked and stuttered, "Ah...mmm...this came to our house by mistake." She thrust a cream-colored envelope toward Sam.

Sam took the letter and glanced down at the familiar stationery. "Thanks. It's a letter from my mother," he explained, placing his hand on the doorknob.

"Your mother?" Merry's blond brows arched high above her blue eyes.

"Yep," he confirmed, keeping a completely straight face despite the exaggerated astonishment comically displayed on Merry's face. *The kid must think I sprang from under a rock.* "She's a nice woman. I think you'd like her, and I'm sure she'd like you. Next time she comes to Rhodesboro, I'll make sure you meet her."

"I'm sure I'll like her. *Your* mother would have to be wonderful," Merry gushed. Her heavily mascaraed lashes batted seductively.

Suddenly comprehension dawned. He was being hit on by a girl who was young enough to be his daughter! Sam managed to cover his dismay with a modicum of finesse, and then the ringing of his telephone provided the perfect excuse to terminate Merry's visit. "Oops, there's the phone. Thanks for bringing this over, Merry. Say hello to your mother for me." He backed quickly through his doorway.

Sam was able to deliver his greeting to Sharon personally a short time later when he was returning from his weekly appointment with Mrs. Krouse's cat, Boris.

That cat had indirectly saved him from one Markovski woman only to literally throw him in the path of another.

As he walked briskly past his neighbor's garage, he was totally involved in questioning the wisdom of having left his ladder leaning against Mrs. Krouse's tree. Having finished the steps to his sleeping loft two evenings before, he'd had no further use for a ladder that high. So, after shouldering the heavy thing and carrying it down the long driveway, across the street and into Mrs. Krouse's backyard, he'd decided to leave it there. Unfortunately, visions of a white-haired lady tumbling down the ladder's wooden rungs were all too vivid. Sam turned on his heel.

"Oops!"

"Whoa!"

Sam's and Sharon's cries were simultaneous, but not uttered in time to ward each other off. Momentum carried their bodies onward in their collision course, only a frail brown paper sack buffering the unavoidable impact. Instantly the overflowing grocery bag split and gave up its contents.

A dozen lemons bounced like tennis balls on the sidewalk and rolled into the grass. Aluminum cans clattered to the driveway. Two loaves of bread were compressed to a doughy mass despite a last-minute attempt to save them from a similar fate.

"Oh, I'm so sorry—"

"My fault, I turned back and didn't—"

"No, it's all my fault. I wasn't watching where I was going," Sharon insisted, transferring the oddly shaped bread loaves to the crook of one arm. She took a step backward to survey the whereabouts of her groceries. "Oh, Sam, your shoes!"

A carton of eggs had flipped open on its downward flight and deposited its contents on Sam's feet. Looking down, Sam saw the instant omelet oozing over his shoes and soaking through his socks. He lifted one loafered foot and watched the slithery mass dribble from the rich cordovan leather. "Uh...that'll really give 'em a shine."

His smile died when he looked into Sharon's face. "Sharon...?" Her huge eyes were brimming with tears, and her lower lip was quivering. "Hey! It's only a dozen eggs. I'll go get some more," he offered in an attempt to soothe her.

"All those eggs...your shoes...Merry's turned into a vamp...Michael thinks he's the boss...Tim won't talk...the noise...always bugging you..." she babbled incoherently, while tears flowed down her cheeks and she squeezed the rest of the life out of the bread. "No wonder you want nothing to do with me."

The words were out before Sharon could stop them, and she would have given anything to take them back. Ever since their walk and their painfully honest discussion about the future of their relationship, she'd thought of little else but her attraction to Sam. Her response to his kisses had been revealing enough. The last thing she'd wanted to do was act as if his rejection had any lasting effect on her.

She'd intended to keep up a friendly front. She wouldn't allow him or anyone else to know that she'd tossed and turned each night as dreams of him brought her awake, or that her pulse raced every time she saw him.

Now, the very first time she'd run into him she'd thoroughly blown her cover. Their collision was the last straw in what had been a trying day from the start.

After another restless night she'd had one run-in after another with her three teenagers. Michael, finding himself an overnight "big fish in a little pond," had let his newfound popularity go to his head; he seemed to think he need no longer take any orders from his mother. Tim had been so reclusive, she'd had to threaten violence to get him out of his room. And then Merry had tearfully accused her mother of being intent on ruining her daughter's life when Sharon objected to the amount of makeup the thirteen-year-old had heaped on her face.

Even Theresa, usually so emotionally steady, had snapped a time or two—a sure sign that she was about to join her elder siblings in the mystical land of adolescence. Sharon had felt more and more inept all day. Her overwrought nerves coupled with three nights of sleeplessness had brought her to the breaking point.

Sam watched in total dismay as Sharon seemed to crumble before him. Nothing she said made any sense. Instinctively he wanted to cuddle her and protect her from whatever had thrown her into such a state. He plucked the tattered grocery sack and the remnants of two loaves of bread from Sharon's arms, tossed them aside and gathered her to him. "Now, now, sweetheart. Everything will be okay," he soothed, holding her close. "Please, this is not the end of the world. My shoes will recover."

"I know." Sharon snuffled against Sam's chest, trying desperately to stop the tears. However, being held in Sam's arms, feeling his hard strength, hearing his gentle words of reassurance, and breathing in the unique scent of him, made it all the more difficult to stem the tide. It felt far too good to be in his arms, and now her tears were for what might have been and never would be.

His cheek resting on the top of her head, Sam rubbed one palm in a slow circle over her back, trying desperately not to press her closer. He chuckled inwardly when he realized how grateful he was that a dozen eggs had fallen onto his feet. It had provided him with a good excuse to hold her, bury his nose in her hair, breath in the sweet, feminine scent of her and enjoy for at least a few minutes how perfectly she fit against his body.

"Do you always cry over broken eggs?" he asked, hoping to stop the flow of tears that was totally unmanning him.

A sob shuddered through her body. "Never before," she choked out, getting herself under control. "It's ridiculous, but I never spilled a whole dozen on a man's feet before, either. I'm really sorry." She straightened her spine resolutely.

Sensing her withdrawal, Sam gave her a little hug, kissed the top of her head, then reluctantly let her move a little away from him. Tipping up her chin, he smiled down at her and said, "It was an accident, but I'll let you redeem yourself by coming over and keeping me company while I scrub my shoes off."

Looking up into the smiling warmth of Sam's eyes, Sharon couldn't resist his invitation. Spending time alone with him might be a mistake, but she was tired of always having to take the future into consideration with every decision she made. Frustrated desire was pure hell, and maybe a flaming affair was exactly what she needed. She did know she needed to get away from her children for a little while and be in the company of another adult.

She supposed she could talk it all out with Aunt Di, and no doubt the woman would be understanding and helpful, but Sharon felt an almost desperate need for a male shoulder right now. "I'll meet you at your house in a few minutes," she said as she stooped down and began gathering up her scattered groceries.

It wasn't very much later that Sharon was inside the carriage house, accepting a glass of chilled wine from her barefoot host. She took a refreshing sip of the tangy liquid. "Tim's hosing off the driveway, and Michael's gone to the store for replacements."

"Feeling better?" Sam asked, and Sharon was aware that she'd upset him with her tears. Perversely, she was almost glad. He'd been as much at fault as anyone.

After all, if she'd had some decent sleep, she probably would have dealt with the kids better.

Sharon settled back against the couch cushions. "Much. How are your shoes?"

"Good as new. See for yourself." With a nod of his head, Sam directed Sharon's attention to the bar. His shoes, cleaned off and polished, rested on a sheet of newspaper.

"Thank goodness. At least one thing's gone right today." She took another fortifying sip of wine. "I don't know why I reacted like that." It was only half a lie. She couldn't admit the full truth; he would take off running.

Sam lowered himself to the chair nearest her. Her eyes were still a little puffy, and there were slight shadows under them. "You seem tired. Maybe you're doing too much," he suggested, feeling real concern for this woman who looked as if she was carrying far too much responsibility on her slender shoulders.

Closing her eyes and leaning her head back, she sighed. "I'm not really. We're pretty well settled in. Aunt Di has kept her cleaning service, even stepped it up to once a week. I'm not working, and I have less to do than I did in Pittsburgh. There's no real reason for me to be overtired." *Except that I can't sleep without dreaming such vivid dreams about you and me that I wake up exhausted.*

"You worried about your kids?" *Or are you having the same trouble sleeping that I am?*

Sharon opened one eye. "Let's just say, some days motherhood doesn't have a lot going for it. I don't know why it's surprising that I bawled my eyes out over a dozen broken eggs. What can you expect from a woman whose IQ is hovering around zero?"

Sam choked on his wine. He knew from her tone that the line wasn't entirely humorous. His expression serious, he tried for some understanding of what she was saying. "I think I remember a certain lady in Chicago going through a moron stage."

"Humph." Sharon took another sip of wine and studied her empty glass. Letting Sam think her ludicrous babbling and emotional breakdown had been caused solely by her children was a handy excuse. Maybe she did have a little intelligence left. "Did she ever regain her wits?" she asked, her expression totally deadpan.

"After her son grew up, the woman turned into a genius." Sam picked up the bottle of wine he'd place on his makeshift coffee table and refilled both their glasses. Though he felt a small stab of disappointment that he wasn't the cause of the lavender shadows under Sharon's eyes, genuine concern for her prompted him to continue their conversation on the same subject. She needed an ally, right now, someone to talk to, not someone adding to her emotional problems.

He sat down next to her and put his arm around her shoulders. "Rough day, Mama?" he asked, determined to offer her comfort and absolutely nothing else.

"You could say that." Sharon snuggled comfortably against him and took a sip from her refilled glass, welcoming the relaxing effects of the wine. She knew from past experience with wine that her capacity was one glass. If she finished another glass, she'd become a blabbermouth and reveal anything that passed through her befuddled mind. She took another long sip of the delicious vintage, well on her way to finishing the second glass.

"Want to talk about it?" Sam gulped down half his glass of wine, hoping it would dull his senses. Instead, it eroded all his good intentions. His hand, seemingly by its own volition, moved to Sharon's head, pushed it down on his shoulder and remained curved over her hair. His wayward fingers played through her curls.

"Nope," Sharon said staunchly. "You don't want to get involved with a big family, remember?" She drained her glass and held it up to Sam with an appealing smile.

Sam winced. "I remember, but I also remember asking for friendship. A friend listens to problems and, my friend, I'm guessing you've had some today."

"I don't want to talk about it." She dangled the empty glass beseechingly. "Can I have some more?"

Sharon's speech wasn't slurred, just belligerent, a tone he'd not heard from her before. "You're sure you want more?"

"I'm sure," she stated firmly, a set look about her lips.

Against his better judgment, Sam leaned forward and reached for the bottle. As he filled her glass, Sharon reaffirmed, "I don't want to talk about kids. I want to talk about us."

"I see." Nonplussed, Sam handed her the requested refill and set his half-finished glass down. She had to be drunk or well on her way, judging from the defiant lift to her chin. He had the strong feeling one of them had better remain sober. If he were really a gentleman, he'd cut her off, but curiosity won out over nobility. "What about us?"

Sharon straightened. Scooting a little forward on the couch, she turned and looked him straight in the eyes. "How do you know I can't handle an affair?"

Sam gulped down the stunned lump in his throat. "An educated guess?" he managed, beginning to feel sorry he'd indulged his curiosity.

Sharon stared at him, her expression thoughtful as she started in on her third glass of wine. As soon as her taste buds made contact with the spirits, she held the glass away from her and frowned down at the pale liquid. It no longer tasted quite as good as it had.

"You've known a lot of women, I suppose," she said, leaning across him to place the glass on the stack of boxes serving as an end table.

"I've come across a fair share in my thirty-eight years," he admitted warily, anticipating her falling against him. Though obviously tipsy, she managed to keep her balance and the steadying hands Sam placed on her waist were impatiently brushed aside.

She shook her head slightly to clear it, glaring at the smirk on Sam's face. "Fair share? What does that mean? Hundreds? Thousands?"

"Hardly," he scoffed. "I haven't been a monk, but I'm not superman."

"But you have *known* a lot of women, haven't you?" Sharon demanded stubbornly, her emphasis indicating what she really meant.

"Not a lot, sweetheart. I've known some," he acknowledged, growing increasingly more uncomfortable under her interrogation. He'd anticipated finding out what was going on inside her pretty head, not being pumped about his past.

"Were you friends with any of them?" she asked, her torso weaving slightly forward and backward. She placed her hands on his shoulders to steady herself.

"I have had and still have quite a few women I count as my friends," he replied honestly.

"But some of them were lovers," she asserted, probing his face with troubled dark eyes.

"As well as being friends." Sam supplied the information slowly and with a great deal of reservation. She was staring at his mouth with provocative intent. "Sharon . . ." he warned as she leaned forward.

"Sam," she breathed softly.

"Oh Lord." Unable and unwilling to stop her, Sam didn't move away as Sharon's lips descended unerringly to his.

Her inhibitions washed away by the wine, Sharon teased Sam's lips with the tip of her tongue. She traced their shape, and then remembering the enthralling sweetness of his kisses, sought entry into his mouth. With a low groan, Sam gave up any resistance and opened to her. With reckless abandon, Sharon explored the tantalizing interior and unwittingly drove Sam closer to the edge of control.

Sliding her tongue along his, she invited his response and received it. When she moved her hands from his shoulders to frame his face, Sam wrapped his arms around her and gathered her against him, enticed beyond endurance.

Thrusting his tongue past hers, he swept through her mouth, drinking her sweetness. He shifted their bodies until they were half lying on the couch. Sharon welcomed the weight of him over her and wrapped her arms around his shoulders, pulling him closer. She gave him all he asked for and more, but also took for herself. Hunger and satisfaction combined to produce more hunger, and demand even more satisfaction.

When at last Sam found the will to lift his lips from hers, she caught his face between her hands. Holding him motionless, she asked, "Do you still want only to be my friend?"

Startled out of the sensual stupor she'd created, Sam stared down into her face, taking in her flushed cheeks, slightly opened lips and lambent eyes. "No."

"Make love to me, Sam," she whispered.

"No," Sam stated gently but with painful finality.

Sharon felt chilled. All the pleasurable sensations that had been coursing through her came to a sudden stop. "Don't you want me?"

Sam kissed the tip of her nose, her temple, and then nuzzled her ear. It was all he could do not to succumb to the rampaging fever she'd inspired in him. He could have her. He could have her right now. He sighed regretfully. "I want you, sweetheart, but not tonight."

Sam knew he should put action to words. But what would it hurt to hold her just a little longer, savor her sweet body beneath him for another moment or two? He rationalized his reluctance to let go with the idea that continuing to hold her would soften his denial of her request to make love to her.

"Are you still worried about all those strings attached to me?" she asked, squirming when his lips grazed behind her ear.

"No," he answered in a choked growl. "And for heaven's sake be still." Her writhing movement beneath him had nearly cost him his resolve.

Sharon froze at the curt order. Tempting fate one last time, Sam brushed his mouth across her lips, then pushed himself up and away from her. "Right now, your kids are the furthest thing from my mind."

Sharon swung her feet to the floor and sat up. Her large eyes were full of puzzlement and hurt. She was also feeling very sober and suffering the beginnings of acute embarrassment. She had practically attacked the man!

Sam read the range of her emotions correctly. He stood up and extended his hand to help her up. Wrapping her in a gentle embrace, he said, "You told me once that I was a gentleman. A gentleman doesn't take advantage of a lady who's had too much wine."

"That's kind of you to hand me an excuse, but I wasn't drunk," she said, keeping her gaze centered on the buttons of his shirt.

"No, but you weren't quite yourself," he said, rocking gently in a comforting motion intended to soothe them both.

When the even beat of his heart matched hers, Sam escorted her out the door. Neither spoke as they walked down the driveway toward her house. After what had just happened, it was an oddly companionable silence.

At the back steps, Sharon turned and smiled up at him. "Thanks, Sam."

"If you really want to thank me, you can go out with me tomorrow night," he returned.

"As a friend?" she asked, unable to help herself.

"Let's play it by ear, okay?" he said, and dropped an all-too-brief kiss on her lips.

6

IN THE DUSKY LIGHT of evening, Sam directed Sharon's attention to the spot where his family's ancestral home had once stood. Like the Rhodes house, it had been built decades before, but unlike its neighbor, it had been left unoccupied after Sam's grandparents had died. Then, before Sam's father could decide what to do with the house, nature had stepped in and taken the decision out of his hands. Lightning had struck the house, and it had burned to the ground.

"I played around with the idea of rebuilding it when I first moved back here," Sam said, catching Sharon's elbow to keep her from tripping as they tramped around the ruins. "I had a lot of happy memories of that place and how beautiful it was. I guess I thought I could make it rise like a phoenix from the ashes."

Sharon empathized with Sam's feeling of loss for the house that he'd once loved. As he described it, it had had three floors, hand-carved woodwork and imported Italian marble fireplaces. A stained-glass window had filled the stairwell between the first and second floors. It had been his home until he was five, at which time his father had taken a position with a large, prestigious law firm in Chicago, the same one Sam had joined and since left. "What changed your mind?" she asked.

"Practicality." He stopped to give Sharon a moment to shake a pebble from her shoe. "In the first place, it would have been impossible to duplicate all the materials and the workmanship. In the second place, it would have been a total waste for me to build myself a six-bedroom house to ramble around in. The carriage house is far more suitable for my needs. I'm lucky Diana was willing to sell it to me before I got carried away with the idea of rebuilding the old homestead."

Sharon interpreted Sam's comments to be a reminder that he enjoyed living alone and intended to continue doing so. She warned herself to keep that in mind and not expect him to change. He'd be her friend, possibly her lover, but nothing more.

"It's a pretty setting," Sharon commented wistfully, directing her thoughts back to her dusk-shrouded surroundings. Ancient oaks, sycamores and maple trees dotted the property. Though weeds and bare patches dominated, Sharon could imagine a yard that had probably once been as impeccably groomed as her aunt's.

As they tramped around the property, Sam swung their hands companionably between them. Sharon felt good knowing that his strong arms were there to steady her when the footing was rough, both literally and figuratively.

Whether he remained her friend or became far more to her, it didn't matter. Somehow, she knew he'd always be a source of strength, whenever she needed it. Something had drawn her to him right from the beginning, something more than the desire aroused by physical attraction. She hadn't gone out with a lot of men since Mike's death, but enough to know that Sam was very special.

Suddenly aware that she'd been paying absolutely no attention to whatever Sam had been saying, but guessing that it had something to do with the youth-center project he'd brought up during dinner, she asked, "What made you decide to donate the land for a youth center?"

Sam kicked at a clump of weeds pushing through what had once been a flagstone walkway. "Family tradition, maybe. The college, even the first grammar school, was set up by a Jefferson. This plot of land is an ideal location for a youth center. It's within walking distance of the school. It's at the end of a street, and the woods will buffer some of the noise the kids will make."

"Sure the neighborhood wants all the kids in town coming and going at the end of this block?"

"Didn't you notice that the building is to be at the farthermost corner of the lot?" he countered. "That was one of the stipulations for getting the council's approval. I might add that as long as we can hear 'em, we have some idea what they're doing."

Sharon chuckled. Not for the first time, she wondered why Sam didn't think he could fit the role of father. Even he admitted he liked kids—at least he said he liked hers. But then she knew better than anyone that there was a big difference between working with teenagers, liking them, being around them and actually living with them. "You know kids pretty well, don't you?"

"Have to," Sam replied with a grin. "I've discovered I really like being mayor of this little town and those kids are future voters."

"I sure hope they appreciate what they'll be getting."

"Skeptic," he chided, then informed her that a group of high school students had approached the town council with the idea in the first place. They had even promised to provide the labor if the council could provide the land and the materials.

"And so, the very noble and caring mayor did," Sharon finished the story for him.

"It's not an altruistic gesture by a long shot. I get a nice tax write-off out of the donation."

"Not that much. Giving this land to the town specifically for the kids' use is very noble and caring," Sharon maintained firmly.

"Noble and caring, that's me," Sam said, the weight of Sharon's estimation becoming an ever heavier burden. First, she'd declared him a gentleman, and now she was making him sound like a saint. While he was entertaining continually unsaintly thoughts about what he'd like to do with her, she was attesting to his virtue. The irony of the whole thing was, he honestly liked knowing she had such a high opinion of him—just not quite that high.

At the edge of what had once been the lawn, Sam turned and faced the overgrown lot again. He pointed out where he envisioned the building, patio space and outdoor recreation areas. "It sounds ideal," Sharon remarked, shaking another pebble from her shoe. "When does construction start?"

"We're hoping to break ground in another week or two," he announced with obvious pride.

Sam had started talking about the youth-center project during dinner and when he'd captured her interest fully, he'd suggested they take a look at the eventual location. That had seemed a feasible idea at the time, but Sharon hadn't expected to actually walk around the site. However, Sam's excitement had been infectious, and she'd been swept along.

"Maybe we should have come out here before dinner when there was more light," he suggested, eyeing the dainty, open-toed sling-back Sharon was slipping from her foot.

"And you should have warned me so I could have brought a pair of hiking boots," Sharon teased. Leaning against Sam, she balanced on one foot and shook the other shoe out.

"Coming here tonight was definitely not one of my better ideas," he decreed in self-condemnation. Glancing at his watch, he brightened. "It's early yet. Let's go back to my place, and I'll show you the blueprints."

Sharon couldn't resist taunting, "Is that anything like inviting me up to see your etchings?"

Sam cast her an exaggerated leer and added an evil-sounding chuckle. "We'll see. Are you coming?"

Sharon paused to consider the invitation and evaluate how much of Sam's theatrics were serious. So far this evening they'd been two friends sharing a meal and discussing a community project. However, once inside Sam's cozy carriage house, the attraction between them—always vibrating just below the surface—might just rise and take over. If it did, was she ready?

She'd thought so the evening before, but that was after two glasses of wine and a day that had been especially trying. She'd wanted escape, no matter how temporary. Tonight? "I start my seminar tomorrow and I planned an early night," she said, deliberately stalling.

"I have a board meeting tomorrow morning, and I'd planned on getting to bed early, too," he countered.

Sharon decided she was being ridiculous, worrying needlessly about what might or might not happen if she was alone with Sam. *Play it by ear.* She recalled Sam's words of the evening before and decided it was time to let nature take its course.

A short time later, they lay side by side on the floor with a set of blueprints spread out before them. "From what I see here, the plans look pretty good." She pointed to a walled-off corner in the main room. "Is this where the pop and game machines will go?"

Sam mumbled a distracted-sounding affirmation.

With the tip of a pencil, Sharon tapped a blue rectangle that was designated a multipurpose room.

"What about expanding this room and making it large enough to use as a gym?"

"Hmmm...?"

Sharon turned and frowned at him. Sam wasn't even looking at the blueprints. She tapped the pencil again. "A gym?" she prompted.

"Sounds good." He took the pencil from her and scribbled a note on the sheet. "I'll check with the contractor." Then tossing the pencil aside, he confessed, "I did have an ulterior motive in getting you over here."

Sharon arched one brow. "Oh, really...?" He'd seemed uninterested in the plans since he'd spread them out, and she was beginning to wonder if she actually had fallen for the old "etchings" routine.

"Yep. Since you've got a vested interest in this place and know a thing or two about teenagers, I wanted you on the youth committee." He sent her a thoroughly self-satisfied grin. "I'd say this evening accomplished that."

Sharon wasn't expecting that motive and was surprised to discover how affronted she felt. In retaliation, she punched him on the shoulder. "Why you... you sneak!"

Sam acknowledged the truth in the accusation with an audacious, toothy grin.

"I should have known, you... you politician." She balled up her fist, intending to deliver another punch.

Sam caught her wrist and pushed her onto her back. Pinning her hands on either side of her head, he loomed over her. "Sometimes one has to resort to underhanded tactics to get what one wants."

Sharon's breath caught when she looked up into Sam's face and saw the teasing light in his eyes disappear. His gray irises turned velvety and dark. "And just how underhanded are you, Mr. Mayor?" she managed, despite the way her senses had overwhelmed her brain the second Sam pinned her beneath him.

"Beyond salvation," he said softly.

Sharon watched Sam's face move closer, his thick, straight lashes shutter over his eyes and the shadows accentuate his cheekbones. Then he was kissing her and she closed her eyes, closed off everything but the pleasure of his lips moving across hers.

Against her mouth, he uttered her name. It was a question and Sharon knew her answer immediately. "Yes."

Sam let go of her wrists and wove his fingers through her hair, cradling her head from the hardness of the floor as his body pressed down on hers. When she lifted her hands to his shoulders and held one palm at his nape, his lips became more insistent. Sharon yielded her mouth willingly. His questing tongue swept through her mouth, sending shivers of desire through her.

Sam rolled to his side, gently pulling Sharon with him. She followed, needing to be close. Sweeping a hand down the length of her back, Sam settled a palm over her hip and pushed her into the hardened warmth of his groin. She didn't draw back but fit herself softly against his aroused masculinity.

Sharon felt a groan rumble from deep in his chest and vibrate against her breasts. Enthralled by it, she answered with a soft moan. He left her mouth to nibble kisses along her cheek and toward her ear.

"Fireworks," he muttered against her skin. "Sweet, irresistible fireworks." His tongue licked the contours of her ear, then he trailed his lips down her throat.

With every brush of his lips, Sharon felt as if her blood was being brought closer and closer to the boiling point. Involuntarily she arched her head backward, giving him freer access to her neck. She trembled when spirals of liquid heat spun from her loins as he rocked his hips rhythmically against hers.

He palmed her breast, his touch warm and arousing as he filled his hand with her. Her nipples perked and thrust against the layers separating them from his flesh. Nimbly his fingers went to work on the crocheted buttons down the front of her sweater, and just as expertly unfastened her bra. He pushed aside the front edges of her top and freed her breasts from their lacey cups. Then, his moist mouth sought and found the treasures that were aching for him.

Giddy with the sensations shooting through her, Sharon emitted a sharp, little cry of pure pleasure as she was rolled to her back again. He tongued her nipples, then brought one fully into his mouth. Never stopping the pleasure-torture he was eliciting at her breast, he lifted himself slightly away from her, pulled his shirt from his pants and unbuttoned it. After favoring her other nipple with like treatment, he slid his moist open mouth up her chest and throat.

When he recaptured her lips, he pressed his bared chest to her breasts. The delicious ravishment of his kiss was enhanced by the feel of his chest hair brushing across her breasts as he moved from side to side. "I want you, Sharon," he rasped against her cheek. "I want to sink into your soft body and be held in your warmth."

"Oh, Sam," she breathed, sliding her hands across his chest. "I want you, too."

He lifted himself up and away from her, then scooped her into his arms. "Not on the floor," he said, his voice husky.

Sharon rested her head on his shoulder, her arms wrapped firmly around his neck. She knew she was playing with fire but was willing to chance being burned. Giving in to their desire for one another felt only natural, and right.

When Sam placed his foot on the first step leading up to the loft, Sharon had a fleeting moment of misgiving. How many discussions had she had with her teenagers about keeping their desires in check? Was she being a hypocrite? But she wanted Sam, wanted him so much.

Sam felt her tension. "Go with your feelings, Sharon. I know we'll be good together. It'll be perfect, as perfect as one of your smiles," he said, and was rewarded with one of the same. In return, his mouth swooped down to capture her smile and coax a loving response.

Sharon gave him that response. When he lifted his lips from hers, she pressed her face against his neck, breathing his scent and tasting his skin with the tip of her tongue. Just because she was a mother, didn't mean she wasn't also a woman. She was an adult woman, ready to accept the responsibilities of her actions and the magnitude of this step. She was going into this with her eyes wide open, knowing full well that there was no lifetime commitment involved. He'd been honest with her, and she was totally honest with herself. She wanted Sam more than she'd ever wanted any man. She wanted, needed, to make love with him.

Sam lowered her to his bed. He came down beside her and swept her half under him. "You fit so perfectly against my body," he said hoarsely, kissing his way down her throat and chest. He flicked his tongue across one of her nipples, and Sharon gave a long, pleasure-filled sigh.

Rising to his knees, he quickly undressed her and sat back on his heels, openly admiring her body. He found it hard to believe she'd borne five children. Her breasts were so creamy and high, not large, but perfect for his hands and mouth. Her belly was smooth, slightly rounded but firm. Her hips flared in a gentle curve to her thighs—again smooth and firm. She was so utterly soft.

His body grew languid at the realization that soon he'd be surrounded by all that softness. The gleaming chestnut curls crowning her head, her gentle brown eyes, the totally kissable mouth and glorious body—she was the essence of soft femininity, and for at least right now, she was his.

His eyes were dark with desire when he looked down at her, and Sharon glowed inwardly from his adoration and the knowledge that her body pleased him. He rose from the bed, his eyes never leaving hers as he shed his clothing. "You are so beautiful," he said huskily. Then gloriously nude, he stood before her.

Sharon caught her breath. Only the glow from the main room below gave any light to the loft, but it was enough. "You're beautiful, Sam," she replied in open admiration for the man within as well as the magnificent physique that housed him.

His shoulders were wide and squared, wrapped in lean muscle. His chest was partially camouflaged with a pattern of dark curling hair, wide and thick across his pectorals, then narrower and thinner down his lean abdomen. His legs were straight and long muscled, exquisitely masculine in their shape. His desire for her was blatant and powerful, the sight heating Sharon's entire body and weakening her limbs.

"We'll be beautiful together," he promised as he lowered himself upon her.

Sharon could only murmur and sigh his name over and over again as he caressed her and scattered light kisses over her face, neck and shoulders. He smoothed his palms down her torso, her legs and inside her thighs. As Sam familiarized himself with every secret of her body, he delivered huskily pronounced compliments about the texture of her skin, her scent, her curves. He sensually described the effect each was having on him and what he was going to do about it. His fingers tantalized her, bringing her close to climax, then soothing her.

Writhing beneath his touch, Sharon needed to discover him as he was discovering her. She moved her hands over his shoulders, back, chest, exploring and caressing every inch of the muscles girding his long frame. They rippled and tensed beneath her touch, and Sam's breath quickened as she moved closer to that part of him that yearned the most for her. Returning some of the tormenting delight he'd given her, Sharon teased him with her fingertips, then retreated until Sam could stand it no longer and begged her to hold him.

They were both quivering when Sam kneed Sharon's thighs apart and settled himself between them. He joined their bodies swiftly and deeply, but when he felt the unexpected tightness of her body and heard the sharp intake of her breath, he stayed the driving motion he craved. Supporting himself on his forearms, he studied her face for any sign of what was wrong.

Sharon opened her eyes and saw the worried furrow on Sam's face, the tautness in his features resulting from restraint. "I'm fine . . . it's been a long time," she assured him, a tentative smile lifting the corners of her mouth.

"I don't want to hurt you," he vowed, the effort to withhold himself evidenced by the shakiness of his speech.

"You won't." She pulled his head down and kissed him, loving him all the more for the care and gentle concern he was showing for her. "Love me, Sam . . . please," she urged.

Taking care, he moved slowly at first. Then, when she answered and lifted to meet him, he moved more rapidly, escalating and spiraling them toward the heights of pleasure. Sharon cried out her joy when a heated tension started at her center and spread outward, breaking when it reached the peak and leaving her awash with satisfaction. One last, deep thrust, and Sam joined her.

Perspiration had formed a light sheen on their bodies and their breathing came in halting gulps as they held each other in the aftermath. "You were right," Sharon whispered weakly, never having felt so blissfully satisfied.

"About what?" he asked as, keeping their union, he rolled to his back carrying her with him until she lay sprawled atop him. Shoving his long fingers into her hair, he tugged her down for a kiss.

"It was beautiful," she said when he released her mouth and her breathing had calmed.

Tucking her head in the curve of his shoulder, he corrected her. "We were." He smoothed his palms in circles over her back. "We were incredible."

"Incredible," Sharon echoed sleepily, swirling the tip of her finger absently around Sam's ear.

Sam caught her hand and brought her palm to his lips. He placed a gentle kiss there. "Thank you," he said reverently, overcome by the special gift she'd just given him. She was young, healthy and capable of great passion, yet there had been no one else during the years of her widowhood. He reaffirmed his earliest estimation of her.

Sharon didn't take sex casually, nor was intimacy with her something he could take lightly. Feeling fiercely protective and responsible for her, he folded his arms around her and held her close. His desire for her renewed, and he felt himself growing inside her, reaching for more of her. "Oh Lord," he vowed when he felt her tremble. "Once might never be enough with you."

It was a long time later before they pulled away from each other and returned to a world full of other obligations. The temptation to remain in Sam's bed until dawn was overwhelming, but Sharon knew she couldn't. She had to get home, even if home was only a short walk away.

Once they were dressed, Sam came up behind her and turned her into his arms. Wrapping her warmly against him, he declared, "One more for the road."

He kissed her so heatedly Sharon nearly melted to the floor and begged him to make love to her again. He tore his lips from hers and, with unsteady hands, set her away from him. "I think I'd better get you home right now or I'll skip my meeting, and you'll be taking part in an entirely different seminar."

Still shaken by their final embrace, Sharon wasn't able to form coherent words. She was gratified by the shakiness in Sam's voice and hands that told her he'd been similarly affected. No matter what happened, she would never forget what had transpired between them this night.

With Sam's arm draped around her shoulders and Sharon's wrapped around his lean middle, they walked the short distance to her home. They didn't speak, but enjoyed the quiet of the night and the closeness of each other. Without a word, he reached again for her when they arrived at her back steps.

Once again, his kiss was so demanding Sharon felt her whole body melt. Trembling, she was oblivious to everything but the possession of his mouth, the wild sweep of his tongue and the delicious taste that was his alone. Against her lips, he invited, "To hell with seminars and meetings. Come back with me and spend the night in my arms."

The kitchen light came on, and the sound of voices intruded on the warm cloud of desire that had cushioned Sharon from everything but Sam. "I can't." Reluctantly she slipped out of his arms, turned away and started to mount the steps.

Sam caught her hand and abruptly halted her flight. "I guess I forgot about your kids."

"Well, I can't ever forget about them. They're very much a part of who I am," she told him, furtively looking over her shoulder to make sure they weren't being overheard.

"Don't you ever forget them?" he asked, his gaze intense and searching.

Sharon shook her head.

"Not even when we made love?"

His question stabbed through her; she felt wounded. "Don't you know the answer to that?"

Sam closed his eyes for a moment. "Sorry, that was unfair of me. I had all of you for a while, didn't I?" His arms came around her, and he dropped a soft kiss on her mouth.

"Yes, you did," she whispered, and swayed against him, her arms locking around his waist.

He held her close, his cheek resting on the top of her head. "I know I'm being an egotistical bastard, but I needed to hear you say that."

Beyond the back door, Michael and Tim were arguing over the merits of chocolate sauce versus butterscotch. Merry's voice joined those of her brothers. Sharon's world. A world of growing, tumbling girls and boys struggling toward adulthood. It was the one she knew, and it would still be there tomorrow. She was a stranger to the world Sam had just given her a glimpse of, and she didn't know how long he'd be willing to guide a complete novice.

By the light from the kitchen, Sharon could see the invitation still being issued in Sam's eyes. She shook her head and curved her hand to his jaw, whispering his name. He turned his face and kissed her palm lingeringly before stepping away. "Tomorrow night, then," he said, and was gone before she could confirm or deny the assignation.

Sharon hesitated at the back door, wishing three of her children weren't seated around the kitchen table wolfing down mountains of ice cream. She touched her lips, knowing they were swollen and no doubt redder than normal. Wondering if her children would notice any other differences in her appearance and guess at the reason, she considered tiptoeing off the porch and going around to the front door in the hopes that she could sneak undetected into the house.

"Hey, Mom's finally home," Michael announced, his booming voice cutting easily through the screen door.

Sharon took a deep breath. There was no easy escape now. Giving her hair a smoothing pat, she pulled open the door and went inside. Her eyes blinked as they adjusted to the bright light in the kitchen.

"Have a nice time?" Merry asked.

"Sure took a long time to eat dinner," Michael commented, and received a jab in the ribs from his sister, along with a pointed reminder that, unlike him, civilized people lingered over meals.

"Sam and I tramped around the old Jefferson place and then came back to his house to discuss the plans for a youth center," Sharon explained. She turned to the sink and poured herself a glass of water, playing for a little time to recover and desperately hoping that the cool water would soothe her heated lips. "Is everybody else in bed?" she asked in an attempt to steer attention away from herself.

"Yeah, we're the only night owls up watching TV," Merry supplied. "Is there going to be a youth center?"

Sharon turned back to face them, leaning against the counter as she finished drinking her water. "Mmm-hmm," she affirmed. "Wait till you see the plans. You're really going to like it."

"Sure must have been fascinating looking at blueprints," Michael commented, doggedly persistent in giving his mother the third degree. He was undaunted by the looks of censure he was receiving from Merry. "Out a little late, weren't you? It's almost midnight, and you start that class tomorrow."

"Mike . . ." Merry warned. "You're sounding like a parent."

"Well I *am* the man of this house," he asserted.

"Self-appointed," Tim gibed sarcastically.

"Neither one of you is a man," Merry stated firmly. "Next to Mr. Jefferson, you're both pitiful."

"Isn't the late movie about to come on?" Sharon asked, in hopes of averting a confrontation. Still glowing and weak from Sam's lovemaking, she was in no shape to act as an arbitrator. Michael took a quick confirming look at the clock over his mother's head and started out of the kitchen.

Sharon halted him. "Your bowl and spoon, Michael." As if he'd never seen it before, he frowned quizzically at the soup bowl with the telltale remains of chocolate syrup dripping down the sides.

"Rinse them and put them in the sink."

Tim was already there with his. "Yeah, macho man. Real men *do* rinse their dishes. You don't ever see any dirty dishes sitting around at Sam's place do you?"

"He doesn't have a woman to take care of them for him," Michael countered, picking up his bowl under the increasingly stormy glare of both his mother and his sister. "What'd I say?" he asked defensively on the way to the sink.

Merry rolled her eyes and shook her head in disgust. "You're such a male chauvinist, Mike!"

"Dad never did dishes," Michael pointed out with painful clarity. "I don't see why I should have to."

"Yeah, well Dad wasn't perfect," Tim inserted sharply. "And you're not him."

"More'n you are, Mr. Wizard," Michael shot back airily as he pushed through the kitchen door.

Sharon saw the shattered look cross Tim's features and felt his pain. "Oh, Tim, he didn't mean that the way it sounded."

"Yes he did!" Tim shouted belligerently. "He looks like Dad, acts like Dad and he's a jock just like Dad was. No matter what I do, I'll never be the kind of son Dad wanted." He bolted toward the back stairs and was gone before Sharon could stop him.

7

SHARON RESTED HER ELBOWS on the kitchen table and leaned her forehead into the warmth of the coffee mug she held in her hands. Getting the good night's rest she'd wanted before starting her seminar had proved to be impossible; responsibility for the welfare and happiness of her children had never weighed so heavily on her mind. There was so much they needed from her. And she didn't know if she had any right to selfishly snatch time away from them. *Oh, Sam, is there any room for you—for us—in my world?*

Last night, her attempts to talk with Tim had left her feeling drained. Tim's closing statement to her had been nothing new. Despite all her reassurances, he clung to the belief that he'd been a disappointment to his father.

Nothing she'd said could convince him that Mike had been proud of his academic achievements, his electronic and mechanical abilities, and that his father had seen him as the very special person he was. Like a hair shirt, Tim had gathered his athletic failures and worn them, doing penance for being different from his father and brother.

When she'd sought out Michael, she'd had little more success. Though he had gone through the motions of acting repentant, Sharon had the distinct feeling she hadn't really gotten through to him, either. Furthermore, he'd adroitly turned the topic of conversation back to her relationship with Sam. Her only deliverance from his cross-examination had come when she'd managed to pique his interest in the youth center.

Sharon had showered and gotten ready for bed, only to lie there feeling as if she was being pulled in six different directions. Sleep had only come in short snatches. Figuratively, her bed had been too full of people for her to relax. Her children's faces and Sam's had swirled around her, each fighting for dominance. In fitful dreams, she had felt like a hapless juggler, trying to keep them all happy at once, but dropping one after another, until they were all broken.

She'd been awake since the sun yawned its first rays into the room. At six, she was at the kitchen table, asking herself the same questions she'd asked the night before and receiving no answers.

Why had Michael been so sullen? She knew he liked Sam but he'd seemed upset that she'd spent more than two hours with the man. Timothy? Her heart ached for him. She had to find a way to prove all the things she'd said to him. Mike had loved Tim as much as he'd loved all his other children.

For the first time since those early months after Mike's death, Sharon was angry with Mike for dying. Tim needed his father! Mike was the one who should be here talking this out with Tim. Instead he'd worked too many extra shifts and ignored the safety precautions until heat and exhaustion had taken a permanent toll.

Mike's motives for all the extra hours, and therefore extra pay, had been to provide all that he thought his family had required. He'd never believed her when she'd said that she didn't need all the luxuries he'd showered on her and the children. For the first time Sharon wondered if Mike hadn't been motivated more by a need to prove to his wife's parents that he was good enough for her than what he wanted to give to his family. For all his burly size, he'd had a fragile ego.

Munching a piece of toast, she decided that she was asking too much of herself, trying to keep everybody happy all of the time. "You're only human," she declared aloud. The soft chiming of the floor clock in the hallway answered her. "Take one day at a time and do your best," she counseled herself.

"Sound advice," Diana Rhodes affirmed as she came down the last three steps of the back stairs. "Are you lecturing yourself or practicing a speech for one of the kids?"

"Myself," Sharon confessed. "Sorry I woke you."

"You didn't," Diana disclosed. She poured water in a small copper teakettle and set it on the stove. "Old folks like me wake up at the crack of dawn even though we've finally earned the right to stay in bed." She pulled a cup and saucer from the cupboard. "It's part of the senior package. Like having to give up coffee and limit your tea. It's a . . . what is it the kids say?"

"A bummer?"

"Bummer. Good word." She plopped a tea bag in her cup and drummed her fingers on the edge of the counter as she waited for the water to boil. "So what's troubling you? Not still worried about moving in here with me, are you?"

Sharon took a last swallow of her lukewarm coffee before answering. "No, you've finally gotten it through my thick skull that you will survive and that you truly want us here." She stared into her mug, studying the design of the sprinkle of grounds. "I'm just worried about being able to spread myself thin enough to satisfy all the people who need me."

Diana grabbed the teakettle when it began to whistle. "Are you including Sam?"

"Sam?" Setting her coffee mug down on the table, Sharon searched for an answer. "I, ah, don't think he needs me," she said slowly. He wanted her, yes. But need? She didn't think so. He was so self-sufficient, she doubted he really needed anyone.

Diana carried her cup and saucer to the table, settled herself onto a chair and took a testing sip of her tea. "I think he does."

"Oh, Aunt Di," Sharon scoffed gently, wondering why Diana was pursuing the subject. "The fact that we've gone out a couple of times doesn't mean anything. Sam's been single all these years, and he's not about to change."

She was lying through her teeth, and she crossed her fingers beneath the table in the hopes that her aunt didn't realize it. She and Sam were hardly sharing a meaningless relationship, but she wasn't about to try to explain it to Diana. What good would it serve to tell the woman that her niece was in love with the man next door, but he didn't, and would probably never, return her feelings?

"I wouldn't be so sure of that," Diana persisted, gazing at Sharon with sharp-eyed intensity.

"We're just friends and chances are, that's all we'll ever be," Sharon maintained, fighting to keep from shrinking under her aunt's piercing scrutiny. She'd never been very good at lying, and at that moment she felt a great need to reach out and measure the length of her nose. "Surely *you* aren't going to give me that old bit about every man needing a good woman and that Sam's been waiting all of these years for the right one to come along?" she asked a bit desperately.

Diana smiled, a tantalizingly enigmatic smile. She resembled the *Mona Lisa*. "Don't dismiss it; it could be true."

"Aunt Di! You? A matchmaker?"

"My dear, I've come to know Sam pretty well in the three years he's lived here. That man is searching for something, and he found only part of it when he moved to Rhodesboro. I think you're searching, too. Maybe you'll find what you need in each other."

Before Sharon could assimilate her aunt's statements and respond, Diana abruptly pushed back her chair. She announced that she was going to bathe and get ready for her day. Once again Sharon was alone in the kitchen with only the distant ticking and occasional chime of the hall clock for company. She poured herself another cup of coffee and tried to clear away the cobwebs in her sleepy brain.

BEROBED IN WEATHERED BRONZE and standing on an engraved pedestal, Rufus Isaac Jefferson smiled benevolently down at Sharon. From her spot on a courtyard bench beneath the cooling shade of a tree, Sharon smiled back at the statue. Considering the desolate mood she'd awakened to this morning, her disposition was markedly improved.

Several cups of coffee had fortified her enough so her eyes stayed open during the seminar. She'd used the eight-block walk to the campus to ready her mind for the opening lectures.

The speakers had been interesting and the discussion that followed their presentations lively. At least the first day of the seminar had been all she had hoped for. Several points had been brought up that confirmed Sharon's belief that her choice of career was the right one for her. She was all the more anxious to complete her studies and be able to put the educational theories to work.

Still, as stimulating as the first day's session had been, she'd found her mind wandering all too often to Sam Jefferson and the ecstasy she'd felt in his arms the night before. Incredible didn't seem a strong enough word to describe those hours in his bed. It was as if she'd been introduced to a whole new world of feeling, one she hadn't known existed, and one so shattering in its intensity, she was almost frightened by it.

Her attention was drawn again to the statue of Rufus Jefferson. If the artist who'd rendered the sculpture had recreated old Rufus correctly, he and Sam shared the same facial bone structure: the aristocratic planes, the penetrating eyes and the wide, sensual mouth. Sharon studied the statue's eyes.

Was it a trick of the light, or had the artist managed to put a twinkle in those eyes? She wondered if they had been dark gray, like Sam's. Eyes magically able to sparkle with warmth and life, though their color was identical to that of cold, tempered steel.

Had Rufus's voice been smooth and flowing, wrapping around a woman until she was helpless to resist anything he requested? Had he been able to make a woman forget everything, think of nothing but him when she... Lord! She was speculating about a bronze statue's love life!

Benevolence might be a characteristic of the Jefferson family, but she was sure a devilish gene ran straight down through all the Jefferson men. Being possessed by a demon was the only way Sharon could explain the way she'd been so overcome with passion the night before. She had responded and even taken the initiative in reaching staggering heights with Sam. Her body tingled anew and grew warm at the memories of all they had shared.

"Mind if I share your bench?" a feminine voice asked.

"Certainly not," Sharon said, glad for the company. Anything that could divert her thoughts from last night was a welcome relief. She picked up her notebook and purse to make room for the woman.

"You're Mrs. Bennett, aren't you?" Sharon asked, recognizing the tall, stylish redhead as having been one of the speakers from the seminar. "I'm Sharon Markovski."

"Diana Rhodes's niece, right?"

Sharon nodded.

"It's nice to finally meet you, and please call me Arlene. I've been meaning to get over and introduce myself." Arlene settled herself on the stone bench and slipped her shoes off. "That feels heavenly. I've really gotten spoiled this summer, running around barefoot or in sandals. My feet didn't take kindly to being squashed back into regular shoes this morning."

"I know what you mean," Sharon commiserated, moving her feet out from under the bench to show that she, too, was minus her shoes. "How did you know who I was?"

"Nothing slips by unnoticed in this town," Arlene said, and Sharon couldn't help but wince. She wondered how soon the whole town would know that she and Sam were lovers. Quickly she rejected the paranoia, or quite possibly egomania, that made her think her private life was the talk of the town.

"Besides," Arlene continued, totally unaware of Sharon's momentary anxiety, "I saw two Markovskis on the school enrollment for next year, so I had a little edge over some of the other busybodies in town."

"Ah, of course. You're the principal of the middle school," Sharon confirmed, remembering more of Arlene Bennett's introduction at the seminar.

"That's right," Arlene said, shifting her shoulders for a comfortable position against the tree trunk behind the bench. "And you're wondering why I was the speaker on elementary-grades reading methods, right?"

"I . . . well . . . yes," Sharon admitted, deeming any polite fabrication as being unnecessary. "All the other speakers were directly involved with the elementary grades, especially on the primary level."

"I know. I figured the roster needed some variety," Arlene divulged tongue in cheek. Very seriously, she admitted, "I'm a flag-waver about certain educational principles and forced my way into being part of this seminar. I feel very strongly about certain basics that are being skipped over at the elementary level. The little kids here in Rhodesboro are getting a fair background, but from what I hear at state-wide meetings, too many are getting less than they need. I'm all for kids learning to read for recreation, but they can't go through life thinking that's all there is to it. They've got to learn to read for content, even when that content is boring to them."

Arlene snorted with disgust at her own terminology. "Oh, how I hate that word 'boring.' Far too many educators are so fearful they might bore a student, they don't drill them enough. Because of that, kids are hitting middle school and junior high without even an introduction to rules of grammar, spelling, paragraph structure and—"

Interrupting herself with a rueful laugh, Arlene apologized. "Sorry, I do go on. This seminar's provided me with a soapbox, and I'm still fired up. When you get to know me better, you'll find out that I have the tendency to launch into my pitch quite a lot. Actually, this morning wasn't a real honest taste of my usual campaign methods. I managed to keep my comments to a minimum and rather low-key—for me."

"You made a lot of good points during your part of the panel," Sharon told her sincerely. "I know in my own kids' cases, I've not felt they've been drilled enough on the basics."

"Hooray!" Arlene hooted with obvious pleasure. "An ally. You wouldn't like to teach around her, would you?"

"I sure would, but I'll have to wait a year," Sharon said. "I've got to graduate and get my certificate before I can apply anywhere. I start full-time classes here at Jefferson in the fall."

Arlene whistled softly. "For a woman with five kids, that's a lot to take on," she said, but admiration was clear in her expression.

"You know about all my kids?"

Arlene nodded with a grin, her hazel eyes sparkling with golden highlights. "Like I said, nothing much goes unnoticed in this town. Besides, my husband, Doug, is the high school football coach, and he's got his eye on your son," she revealed. "I think he got a letter about . . . let's see, Michael?"

Sharon nodded confirmation.

"Your boy's former football coach sent Doug a letter all about him, and my husband is frothing at the mouth in anticipation of the coming season. Life loses all meaning for him if he doesn't go into the first game with a great backfield."

The two women chatted on, discovering they were kindred spirits on a number of things. It was the kind of conversation Sharon had missed since she'd left Pittsburgh. Just as her children had, she'd left good friends behind.

"Aha! Just the two lovely ladies I wanted to see," a very familiar male voice cut in.

"Sam!" Arlene greeted warmly. "I'd say it's good to see you, but I suspect an ulterior motive lies behind that charming smile you're trying to dazzle us with." In a stage whisper to Sharon, she said, "Watch out for this man. He's pretty hard to resist."

Don't I know it. Sharon's pulse had already speeded up at the sound of Sam's voice. Looking at him made her heart palpitate and her limbs grow weak. It was a good thing she was already sitting down, or she would have slithered to the bricks on which her stockinged feet rested.

He'd slipped off his jacket and was holding it casually over his shoulder. His shirt was crisp and impeccably white, unbuttoned at the throat, and his tie, blue knit and narrow, was loosened. He had one hand splayed over a lean hip, and the sight of his long fingers renewed the sensations that had shot through her last night when he'd explored every inch of her.

It wasn't fair that he should look so fresh and energetic when she felt like an old rag that had been trampled on by a thousand feet. He'd obviously slept well the night before. And why not? she thought. He had no worries except for himself, wasn't being pulled in five—make that six—different directions.

"You wound me," Sam replied to Arlene's jesting attack on his character, feigning an innocence even a two-year-old would question. "Can't you believe I merely prefer the pleasure of your company for lunch over eating with only myself as company?"

"Sure you do," Arlene said sceptically. "Once our mouths are full and we can't talk, you'll have us signed up to serve as chaperons every night of the week as soon as the teen center opens."

Pulling off a convincing look of chagrin, Sam admitted that, though he didn't quite expect that much of a commitment, he did want them both to volunteer to serve the center in some capacity. "How'd you know I wanted to rope you in on the project?" He kept his gaze focused on Arlene, but his thoughts were centered on the petite brunette at the other end of the bench.

"Doug attended the last town council meeting," Arlene reminded him. To Sharon, she explained, "Campaigns run in the family. My husband's been trying to get a teen center going since we moved here. Now that we've got a young hotshot for mayor, it's finally happening."

The carillon chimed the passing of the half hour, and Arlene groped for her shoes. "Sorry, Sam. Maybe you can convince Sharon to have lunch with you but I've got to run. Doug made me promise to rescue him from the children by noon." After a hasty farewell Arlene hurried off, her shoes dangling in her hand.

Sharon slipped her own shoes back on and gathered up her belongings, prepared to follow Arlene's lead. "Let's go," Sam said, cupping her elbow, assuaging his need to touch her. "My car's parked behind the administration building."

"I'm afraid I'm going to have to beg off, too." Sharon said. "I've been gone all morning, and I should check in at home."

"Do you mean that, or are you trying to escape getting even more involved with the teen center than you already are?" He shortened his stride to match hers, but kept on nudging her along. He wasn't about to let her escape. Thoughts of her had occupied so much of his mind all morning that he'd lost his concentration in the midst of a college board of directors meeting and nearly blurted out her name when he'd been asked to vote on an issue.

"I really mean it," she asserted. "You already have my word that I'll do what I can to get the teen center going." She stopped at a junction of bricked walkways, preparing to bid him goodbye and start down the one toward home. "Thanks for the invitation, but I really must go home. I walked, so this is where I'll have to leave you."

"Sharon," he pronounced firmly, his voice wrapping around her the way it always did, especially when he said her name.

She tilted her face up, and Sam felt his body tense. A man could drown in those deep brown eyes of hers, and this man in particular had given up any struggle to keep afloat. "Please? I'd really like to have lunch with you."

"Oh, Sam," Sharon said softly, having trouble resisting his tender entreaty. "I'd like that, too, but I honestly need to get home and check on the kids."

Unaware of the vulnerability that shone from her dark eyes, Sharon restated her position. "I thought I made myself clear last night. Those five kids are my responsibility, and I can't shove them in a closet and forget about them whenever the mood strikes me. Surely you can understand that?"

Sam saw the distress flicker across her face, distress that he'd just caused. He could have kicked himself for pushing her so hard. "I do understand, sweetheart. Bear with me. Please?"

Sam took her elbow, more gently this time, and started steering her toward the parking lot. "I'll drive you home, you can check on the kids, then we'll go have lunch. I really need some help on this youth-center thing. You had some great ideas last night, and I'd like to pick your brain some more."

Relenting, Sharon agreed to the ride. What energy she'd gathered up this morning had begun to dissipate and the eight blocks home loomed like eight miles. Lunch with him was probably out, but he'd guess that once they arrived at her house and he heard everyone clamoring for her attention.

The drive was accomplished in less time than it took to walk to Sam's car. Sam accompanied her up the walkway and onto the back porch, where to Sharon's surprise she found the back door locked and the message board dutifully filled with notations.

"Good idea," Sam complimented as he studied the messages. Sharon nodded absently as she took note of everyone's whereabouts and expected times of return. The system she'd designed almost a week ago, when chaos had been prevailing, was working more effectively than she'd ever imagined. Even Dee Dee was taking the arrangement seriously and had scrawled her name under Diana's message that she had taken the youngest Markovski to visit a friend for the afternoon.

"Looks like all your chicks have flown the coop, mother hen," he observed, and started off the porch with Sharon in tow. "Let's take advantage of it."

"Stop! I can't keep up with you," she protested, nearly taking a header off the porch.

Sam scooped her up in his arms. "This better?"

"No! Put me down this instant!"

"Lady, you're disturbing the peace with all that shouting," he warned, and silenced her by covering her mouth with his own. Actually he'd been wanting an excuse to do that ever since he'd heard her enchanting laughter float across the college courtyard.

Sharon's protests died in her throat as his silencing method turned into a sizzling kiss that threatened to disorient her completely. Before he lifted his mouth away from hers, they were at the front stoop of the carriage house. "Sam, what do you think you're doing?" she demanded weakly, confused and gasping for breath.

"I'm taking you to lunch," he told her as he adjusted her in his arms and fished for his key.

"No one who saw you pulling this Rhett Butler routine would ever believe that," she said, but chose not to struggle. All it took was one adoring look from his marvelous gray eyes, and she wanted to be carried away. It wouldn't hurt to stay in his arms just a little bit longer. Her arms tightened around his neck. After all, how many women would have told Rhett to knock it off before he'd reached the top of the staircase?

"Rhett Butler, eh?" Sam cocked one brow in a smug look. Sharon refused to inflate his ego further, remaining silent as he unlocked his door. Once inside, he shouldered the door closed, hero fashion. Still carrying her, he then marched through the main room toward the steps to the loft.

Sharon caught the newel post as Sam began mounting the steps and clung to it with all of her might. "Oh no you don't," she warned, having brought his progress to an immediate, jarring halt. "You said lunch, remember?"

"According to your children's ETA's and my afternoon-appointment schedules, we're both free until two o'clock." He lowered his face toward hers, but Sharon managed to dodge his lips. "Come on, honey," he cajoled with an exaggerated Southern drawl. "You know you'll enjoy this."

"I will not," she maintained stubbornly, her eyes flashing a challenge as daunting as one of Scarlett O'Hara's. She let go of the banister and crossed her arms over her chest. "Now let me down you . . . you scalawag!"

Sam's booming laugh rivaled Rhett's best. And so did his two-steps-in-a-stride ascent of the stairs. "Certainly, my dear," he agreed smoothly. "Anything you say." He tossed her onto the middle of his bed.

Sharon scrambled to the far side and flattened herself against the wall. "Now listen here, Sam Jefferson, this has gone on long enough." She edged along the wall, keeping a wary eye on Sam for any sign of his gearing up to spring at her. "If you think I'm going to . . . what are you doing?"

He slid his tie from under his collar and draped it over the footboard. "I'm stripping down for action." Smiling at her frantic expression, he slowly pulled his shirt-tails from his pants.

"You . . . you put that back on," she ordered as his shirt was draped over the velvet chair beside his bed. "Don't touch your belt!" She flew across the room and caught his hands.

Sam slipped his fingers from her grasp and locked them behind her waist. "If you'd prefer to take my pants off, it's fine with me."

"You never had any intention of having lunch with me or discussing a worthwhile civic project," she complained half-seriously, spreading her hands against his chest to push herself away. The touch of his warm, solid flesh on her sensitive palms, the scent of his woodsy cologne, struck a strong blow against her resistance. Sharon tried not to breath through her nose.

Sam took her defensive breathing pattern the wrong way, "See, you're already panting for me."

"I am not!" Sharon leaned back as far away from his muscular chest as the circle of his arms would allow. "Tell me what my civic duties are and let me go."

"You're doing them," Sam said, bending over her and nuzzling her ear. He nibbled a line down her neck. "You're spending the next hour or so making the mayor very happy."

"Isn't there a law against that sort of thing?" She shivered as he wrapped her closer and flicked the tip of his tongue in the hollow of her throat.

"Only if you were a civil employee, and I were demanding your favors in exchange for job security," he told her as his fingers made short work of the hook and zipper at the back of her skirt. The gayly flowered dirndl slithered to the floor.

"Sam, we can't do this."

"Yes we can." He started on the buttons down the front of her blouse. "All your responsibilities are elsewhere, and you're all mine for a little while. I'm taking advantage of the opportunity. Besides, you look tired. You could use a pick-me-up."

Again, Sharon grabbed at his hands, struggling to halt their progress before a pink cloud of muslin joined the garment already on the floor. "A nap in my own bed would accomplish that quite nicely."

"Love in the afternoon can be very exhilarating."

She held on to his hands, but he managed to free one finger and push it through the gap he'd created in her blouse, then under the lace of her bra. He brushed the tip back and forth over her breast, and Sharon's breath caught in her throat. "This is positively decadent."

"Yeah, we'll probably sink all the way to barbarism," he told her, and took her mouth with masterful persuasion. Taking advantage of the weakness his kiss had caused in her hands, he freed his fingers and sent them nimbly back to work on her buttons. The blouse and then her bra joined her skirt. He started edging them both toward the bed.

"Don't you understand the meaning of the word no?"

"Sure, but you haven't said the word." He toppled them over onto the mattress.

"I . . . most . . . certainly have," she managed weakly as Sam began stringing kisses across the crested peaks of her breasts.

"Nope, all you've done is tell me we can't." He rolled to a kneeling position beside her and within seconds her shoes, hose and underpants flew through the air. He was off the bed almost before her garments hit the floor, stepping out of his shoes and pulling off his socks.

"I'm just proving to you that we can," he said as he shucked his pants and briefs with a speed that Clark Kent would have envied. In one smooth motion he was back on the bed, his body a warm caress as it settled over hers.

"Mrs. Krouse," Sharon pronounced. "She's always on her porch watching everything that goes on in the neighborhood."

"It's Wednesday," Sam muttered between kisses pressed across her shoulders. "She's at the Methodist church serving the Rotarians' lunch."

Sharon squirmed beneath him as his breath blew softly and warmly against the sensitive spot below her ear. "Shouldn't you be there?"

"I'm in Kiwanis, and we meet on Thursdays."

His hands were as busy as his mouth, skimming down her sides, under her hips and cupping her buttocks in his palms. "Put your arms around me, honey," he directed in a thick, rough voice as he lifted her against his hardened manhood. "I need you to hold me as much as I need to be inside you."

Sharon gave in to the hunger he had succeeded in arousing within her and wrapped her arms around his shoulders, melting her body into his. He moved against her, tantalizing her with the press of his male strength to her heated femininity, but preventing their union by keeping her locked between his thighs. A bittersweet ache began deep within her, and she whimpered her torment.

"That's it, sweetheart, need me as much as I need you." Sam's words were a raspy whisper. He slid his body down hers, lowering his mouth over one aching nipple, drawing it deep into his mouth. As his tongue laved her nipple, his hand stroked down over her stomach to the juncture of her thighs. When he shifted his attention to her other breast, his fingers parted her and slowly, gently probed within.

Coming apart with the onslaught of her need for satisfaction, Sharon began to shake. She lifted her hips from the bed, arching into the pressure of his fingers, involuntarily seeking the ecstasy that was so near.

"Not yet, my sweet love, not yet," Sam crooned, and withdrew his fingers, rocking the heel of his hand against the pulsating delta. He brought her down only slightly, then escalated the torment once more.

"Sam . . ." Sharon cried out for him, but still he refused her. Her arms dropped away from his shoulders as his lips skimmed down her torso finally to replace his hand. He rebuilt the pressure again and again, always raising her, then soothing her until Sharon was so lost, she could think of nothing but Sam and the fulfillment that he promised would come soon.

His name became a sighing plea on her lips until at last he complied with her entreaties. Thickly and deeply, he filled her. "Now, sweetheart, now," he said, moving within her. "We'll go together."

Sharon grabbed Sam's shoulders, clinging for security as he set a driving pace that hurled them both to a swirling vortex of breathtaking sensation. When they trembled at the very brink, they were together, and then they were released, together, to float softly and slowly downward. Sharon cradled Sam's head against her breasts, clinging to him as the pleasure muted and the spirals whirled to a stop.

Finally Sam gathered enough strength to lever himself to his forearms. "That was even more incredible than last night." He dropped a kiss to her nose. "You're incredible."

"Just following orders, your mayorship," Sharon managed breathlessly.

"You're a civic-minded woman," he deemed as he kissed the curve of her shoulder. A low growl came from the vicinity of his stomach. "Since you're so civic-minded, could you fix lunch for the mayor before he dies of hunger?"

"Sam Jefferson, you are the limit!" She pinched him on the behind and had the satisfaction of seeing his smug grin disappear.

8

"HEY, MOM, send me up some nails," Tim hollered from his precarious perch near the ridgeboard of the youth center's skeletal roof.

Sharon tilted her head back and shielded her eyes from the glaring sun. She shuddered, fear prickling down her back when she saw her son's legs dangling through the roof rafters. "Timothy, watch what you're doing!" She kept her eyes on her son as she scooped nails into a pouch.

"Aw, Mom," filtered down through the open roof, and was echoed by a deeper voice beside her. "He's fine. Quit worrying about him," Sam ordered shortly, diverting Sharon's attention away from her son.

Sam took the pouch of nails from Sharon and handed them to Merry. "Take these over to Coach Bennett, Merry," he directed. "He's about to go up to the roof. He might as well take these along with him."

"Tim shouldn't be up there. He's only—" Sharon's protest was stopped by Sam's forefinger pressed against her lips.

"Fourteen," Sam finished for her. "But he's very close to fifteen."

He draped his arm about her shoulders and walked her outside to a quiet spot away from the hustle and bustle of the construction site. Once they were far enough away that they wouldn't be overheard, he said, "Tim needs to be up on that roof."

"*Needs* to be up there?" Sharon was incredulous. "Why can't he be content to be safely on the ground, pounding the sheathing onto the wall studs, like Michael?"

"Because *he* has a choice. Michael doesn't," Sam said very quietly.

"And what does that mean?" Sharon demanded, hands on her hips. "Did you order Michael to stay on the ground and send Tim to the roof, Mr. Mayor?" She sidestepped Sam, obviously intending to countermand any directives he might have given her youngest son.

Sam settled his hands over Sharon's shoulders, exerting firm pressure until she was forced to sit down Indian-style on the grass. Once he was sure she wasn't going to bolt, Sam hunkered down in front of her. "Nobody has been ordered anywhere to do anything on this project. This is a volunteer effort. Everybody's offering their time and expertise wherever it's needed. It so happens that Mike suffers from a little thing called vertigo, whereas Tim has no such problem. Do you understand that, or do I need to spell it out for you?"

"Michael's afraid of heights?" Sharon asked dimly, the news a complete revelation to her.

Sam nodded.

"I didn't know. . . ."

"Neither did he, until yesterday when he volunteered to help put the sheathing on the roof. When he got to the top of the ladder he froze. Tim was the one who went up after him and talked him down."

"How did Michael handle that?" Sharon asked quietly, imagining what a blow to her son's ego the incident must have been.

"Pretty well, thanks to his brother," Sam replied. "Tim's quite a kid."

"Yes, he is," Sharon quickly agreed, springing back to her feet. "But he's still a kid, and he shouldn't be up on that roof."

"Hold it!" Sam ordered firmly.

Sighing with resignation, Sharon sat back down.

"Mike's a kid, too," Sam reminded pointedly. "If he was up on that roof, would you be concerned?"

"No, because he's—" Sharon stopped herself from blurting out that Michael was the oldest and also much bigger and stronger than Tim. Her shoulders slumped. "I haven't been letting Tim grow up, have I?"

Sam nodded. "That's part of it. Though Tim hasn't thrown the vertigo business up to Mike, I have the feeling being able to tackle that roof when his brother can't is proving something to both of them."

Sharon plucked at the grass. "Thanks for stopping me, Sam," she acknowledged graciously. "You're right. Tim has never felt he measured up to his brother. Mike's always been such a jock. It hasn't been easy for Tim."

"I gathered that, but he certainly can't feel inferior around here. He's been a big help. All he needed was a chance to excel at something that requires a little muscle instead of a good head."

"Maybe I have overemphasized his academic achievements," she acknowledged. "Tim's grades have always been so good, I never considered that he might need to prove himself on any other level."

Sam snorted, sitting down beside her. "Us cerebral types need to prove our physical prowess as much as the next guy."

Sharon shook her head. "You men! Why is that so important to you?"

"Why?" Sam thought for a moment, then shrugged. "I suppose what it all comes down to is that a woman doesn't want a wimp in her bed."

"Oh come on."

"Admit it. You love my getting physical."

"There's more to being a man than proving your prowess in bed," she returned primly.

Sam stretched out his legs, crossed his ankles and leaned back on his elbows. "Yeah, but it's a lot more fun than climbing around on a roof."

"Don't spread that information around where my boys can hear you," Sharon advised more seriously than her tone implied.

"Don't worry, Mom," Sam assured. "They won't hear it from me." Crossing his arms beneath his head, Sam lay on the ground. "It's enough for me that *you* know."

Sharon didn't appreciate his self-satisfied grin. Lapsing into a thoughtful silence, she contemplated the difference in their attitude toward sex. Though she had to admit she enjoyed being in Sam's bed every bit as much as he thought she did, she wondered if the thrill of the moment, the fun, was all those encounters meant to Sam.

She was in love with him and from her point of view, married or not, giving less than her all—emotionally and physically—to the man she loved was hypocrisy. However, she was realistic enough to know that others might not see it that way—namely her children and most of the good citizens of Rhodesboro.

She couldn't afford to be labeled the mayor's mistress. In a small town, that kind of reputation would cause considerable damage to both her and her family. Fair or not, Sam didn't have to fear for his reputation. The double standard still applied. A single man could do what he pleased, but a woman, especially a widow with children, had to tread the straight and narrow.

It was becoming more and more difficult to maintain discretion. It was inevitable that, if they continued as they were, their affair would soon become common knowledge. Sam was so open with his affection. In public, he didn't hesitate to hold her hand or drape a possessive arm around her. After the stunt he'd pulled last evening, she was sure tongues were wagging all over town.

Sam had dropped in after dinner and invited her out for a walk. In the pale light of the setting sun, they had ended up making glorious love upon the mossy bank of the creek in the middle of Appleton Woods. Afterward, holding on to the glow that followed, they'd taken a circuitous route home that went directly past Mrs. Krouse's house.

Arms about each other's waists, they'd strolled down the sidewalk. Mrs. Krouse had been seated in a rocking chair on her front porch. Sharon had tried to move to a more circumspect position, but Sam had tightened his hold.

"Wave to Mrs. Krouse, Sharon."

"But Sam . . ."

"Wave to Mrs. Krouse, nod your head and smile," he directed again, and proceeded to follow his own instructions. "There's nothing wrong with an evening stroll, so stop looking so guilty."

"No, there isn't, but that's not all we've been doing." Sharon raised her hand weakly and nodded toward the watchful elderly woman.

"She doesn't know that."

Sharon tried squirming out of Sam's grasp, but again he prevented her escape by tightening his arm around her waist. "Mrs. Krouse is a notorious gossip. Let go of me. Don't you know what she's going to tell people if she sees us together like this?"

"If I don't at least keep my arm around your waist, my hands will stray to where they really want to be, which is inside your blouse, holding those gorgeous breasts of yours," he returned as easily and nonchalantly as if he'd been discussing the weather. "Then she really will have something to talk about." To emphasize his statement, he brushed his thumb threateningly close to the bottom slope of her breast.

Sharon gasped and stumbled. Laughing, Sam hugged her a little tighter.

"You're incorrigible!"

"No, I'm insatiable." He bent quickly and nipped her ear.

Sharon let out a small squeak and spun out of his grasp, only to be caught again by his arm settling over her shoulders. A quick glance across the street confirmed that Mrs. Krouse was still eyeing them with more than a passing interest. "What must she be thinking?"

"Who? Mrs. Krouse?" He reached over to pluck a blossom from a mock orange bush. Beneath the glowing circle from a streetlamp, he tucked the fragrant white flower behind Sharon's ear. "She's been trying to match me up with every available woman in the county since I moved here. Maybe she'll stop if she thinks I've found one."

Sam had hauled Sharon against him, bent her back over his arm and kissed her long and hard. Then, righting the sputtering woman in his arms, he had saluted the white-haired lady who was leaning so far forward in her chair she was in danger of tipping over the edge of her porch. "Nice evening, isn't it, Mrs. Krouse?"

Recalling her embarrassment over the incident, Sharon still felt a flush of heat. Sam hadn't been the least bit embarrassed. He obviously had no qualms about what people might say.

"Hello . . . hello," Sam drawled, his voice bringing Sharon out of her reverie. "That's some frown. You're not still worrying about Tim being up on the roof, are you?"

"Roof?" she asked vacantly, having trouble assimilating the question. "Eh . . . not really. I can appreciate why he's up there. Thanks again for providing him with a chance to prove himself."

"My pleasure. I was once a fourteen-year-old boy myself. Tim and I have a lot in common." Sam paused, then stated more than asked, "Mike's like his dad, isn't he?"

"How did you guess?" She kept plucking at the grass beside her, gazing across the projected parking lot to the building under construction.

"He didn't get all that brawn from you, my little pixie."

"Little pixie?" She looked over her shoulder and scowled. The grin Sam sent her was so charmingly infectious. It went a long way toward dispelling her introspective mood.

"The sexiest little pixie I've ever met," he told her unabashedly, and tousled her hair.

As far as Sharon was concerned, being called a pixie—even a sexy pixie—wasn't much of a compliment. She wasn't very big . . . but a pixie? She pulled up a handful of grass.

"Pixie, huh? I'll show you pixie!" She whirled and caught Sam squarely in the face with her verdant ammunition. Scrambling to her feet, she started to run, but Sam was quicker.

Shaking grass from his face and sputtering it out of his mouth, he jackknifed and caught her around the waist before she made good her escape. A second later, he had toppled her to her back and pinned her on the ground. "Okay, short person. You're about to get your comeuppance."

"Oh yeah?" she challenged, heaving and twisting until Sam had to catch her hands and flatten himself upon her. "Get off me, you big oaf!"

"Not until you pay for that mouthful of grass," he pronounced with demonic glee, and started to lower his head. Sharon struggled all the harder, turning her head from side to side to avoid his kissing her. However, Sam had a different form of retribution in mind. Locking both her hands in one of his, he proceeded to tickle her until she was screeching for mercy.

"Give up?"

"Yes . . . yes . . . stop it!" Sharon cried between bouts of giggles. If anyone saw them carrying on like this, she would be mortified.

"Hey! We could use some help over here," Michael's voice sounded from several feet above them. "Or are you two going to roll around on the grass all afternoon?"

Sharon froze. Opening her eyes, she looked beyond Sam's shoulder to see not only Michael but also Merry and Theresa, staring down at her. The three of them were displaying totally different reactions to the sight of their mother squirming beneath a man and looking like she was enjoying it.

"Oh Lord," Sharon whispered under her breath.

Michael was glowering. Theresa was giggling. Merry's big blue eyes were dark and fathomless as if she was in a state of near shock.

"Break's over," Sam announced smoothly as he rolled away from Sharon and came to his feet. Holding out a hand to help her up, he said, "Back to work, woman."

Sharon grasped Sam's hand as if it was a lifeline. Without it, she was sure she would have lain upon the grass in total embarrassment until the sun went down, maybe longer, possibly until the first snow covered her up and cooled the throbbing heat now reddening every one of her five feet and three inches.

From what seemed a far distance, she could hear Sam giving directions to the children, and their replies. For the life of her, she couldn't make sense of any of it. Her heart was pounding too loudly for her to hear anything else, and her mind was replaying over and over again the expressions on her children's faces.

Michael, Merry and Theresa had gone off to their respective assignments by the time Sharon came to her senses. "Don't look so condemned, sweetheart," Sam soothed as he brushed grass from the seat of her jeans. "It's not the end of the world. They could have caught us in far more compromising circumstances. At least you still had some clothes on."

"Hush," Sharon hissed as she started toward the partially constructed building. "Why don't you just announce to the whole world that we're having an affair!"

Sam reached out and clamped a firm but gentle hand around her arm. Sharon stopped and turned to him, but kept her gaze on the clump of cornflowers crushed beneath Sam's feet. "Oh come on," he scoffed, tipping her chin up. "Don't make more of it than it is, Sharon. That little scene just now was nothing to get so upset about. They'd see far worse at high noon in any city park."

"That may be," she allowed, keeping her gaze directed beyond his shoulder. "But this isn't a big city, Sam. This is a very small town, and we don't act the way you people do in Chicago."

"We?" he queried, failing to keep the humor from his voice and the smile from his lips. "May I remind you that you're even less small town than I am, Miss Pittsburgh. I was born here, and I've been living here longer than you. I think I know this town. After all, I am the mayor."

Sharon's ire had risen a notch with each of Sam's statements. She didn't find the incident at all amusing and finding that Sam did infuriated her. "I don't care if you're the governor of the state," she pronounced, her voice rising. "You don't know this town!"

"And you do?" Sam roared back at her, his humor beginning to dissolve.

"Better than you!" she countered pugnaciously, rising to her toes to meet Sam nearly nose to nose.

"You can run for mayor in the next election," a calmer voice informed Sharon. Diana stepped neatly between the two protagonists and linked an arm through each of theirs. "Seems to me," she continued, "that the best way for you two to let off some steam is to hammer a few nails." Very softly, for Sam's and Sharon's ears only, she added, "Unless you want to continue entertaining all of Rhodesboro."

"Oh no," Sharon gasped out, realizing all activity had stopped and everyone was watching them. Since most of the population had turned out to work on the youth center, they had a large crowd of curious witnesses to their argument. "I'd like to find the nearest hole and jump in."

Sam started chuckling. Sharon would have gladly decked him if her aunt hadn't had a firm grip on her right hook. "Oh shut up," she snarled under her breath.

"Follow Sam's lead, dear," Diana advised, a practiced smile on her face as she walked them toward the building. "Everything will blow over quicker if you make light of it now."

"That's the way things work in a small town," Sam needled, and would have said more had Sharon not sent him such a glare that he quickly shut his mouth. If looks could kill, Sam Jefferson was as good as buried.

Discretion was indeed the better part of valor, Sam decided, and hastily parted company with the two Rhodes women. He joined Tim and several others on the roof and wisely remained there until dusk called a halt to the work for that day.

Sharon gathered up her children and the remnants of the picnic supper she'd brought over. Aunt Di was nowhere in sight, so Sharon assumed she'd already gone. Herding her troops toward home, she was glad to see that Sam was deep in conversation with the Bennetts. With luck she might get past him without his noticing.

A party of six, however, is hard to miss, and Sam was neither deaf nor blind. He waved at her, but Sharon pretended not to see. Right then, she wanted nothing so much as to put a great deal of distance between herself and Sam Jefferson. They had entertained the townsfolk enough for one day, and she had no intention of adding any more grist to the gossip mill. There most definitely would be no evening stroll tonight!

She tried to keep the impatience from her voice as she urged her children to hurry up. Dee Dee, whose energy supply had been depleted long ago, had whined and whined until Sharon had picked her up. She was growing heavier with each passing second. "Michael, you carry your sister," Sharon ordered and thrust Dee Dee at Michael.

"Geez, Mom, what's your problem?" Michael asked sarcastically as he adjusted Dee Dee against his shoulder.

"Your little sister's exhausted and needs to get home and into bed," Sharon snapped. Out of the corner of her eye, she saw Sam still talking with the Bennetts. Michael, oblivious to his mother's impatience, was carrying on a farewell conversation with his adoring harem. "Michael, we have to get going," Sharon ordered through her teeth. "Now!"

"Sorry, girls, got to get the family home. See ya later." The object of the local teenage females' adulation backed away from a tittering trio, turned and started off at a fast jog. Dee Dee was brought out of her sleepy state immediately and set to giggling.

"Michael! Slow down!" Sharon shouted, hard put to keep up with her long-legged son.

"You're the one in a hurry," he threw back at her, but came to a stop and waited for the rest of his family to catch up.

"Giddap, Mike!" Dee Dee urged. "I wanna horsey ride."

Michael started shifting his little sister around to his back, but Sharon quickly halted him. "Oh no you don't! No horsey rides tonight," she informed her youngest. To Michael, she snapped, "Now look what you've done. Dee Dee's all keyed up, and I'll never get her to sleep tonight! Don't you have any sense?"

The minute the accusation was out, Sharon regretted it. Her attack had been unnecessarily sharp and not altogether justified. "Michael, I'm sor—"

He cut her off. "Just because you had a fight with your boyfriend is no reason to take it out on us!"

Even in the dim light of evening, the belligerence in Michael's expression was clear. His statement hung in the air, while his siblings, including the youngest, held their breath waiting for the explosion. Sharon closed her eyes, took a deep breath and let it out slowly.

"I did not have a fight with my boyfriend," Sharon asserted slowly, spacing her words. "I don't have a boyfriend."

"You got another name for Sam?" Michael pressed, displaying a hostility Sharon had never seen in him. "Like lo—"

"Mike, cool it," Tim ordered, attempting to cut off his brother's attack, but Michael's choice of words was clear.

Displaying far more calm than she was feeling, Sharon asked, "Michael, does my seeing Sam bother you?"

Michael didn't answer, and by the set look to his jaw, Sharon knew he wasn't about to. He wore the same expression his father had always adopted when he'd been wrestling with some problem that he couldn't put into words. Sharon felt sick, wondering what was going on in her son's mind, in all of her children's minds. Did they think she was betraying their father? That her relationship with Sam was shameful, tawdry, embarrassing?

Everyone was deathly quiet. Gathering her courage, she addressed them all. "Do any of you disapprove of my seeing Sam?"

After another silence Dee Dee's small voice piped up. "I like Sam."

Then Tim's and Theresa's "So do I" and "Me, too" followed.

But Merry took longer to answer. "I was kind of jealous, Mom," she admitted. "But just for a minute. You know I think it's great you're going with Sam."

Sharon smiled shakily at her daughter, relieved to have her endorsement. She turned to Michael with a hopeful expression. He stubbornly clung to silence.

"Michael?" she prompted, more relieved than she could say that only one of her five appeared to have reservations concerning her relationship with Sam.

Again Michael didn't answer, but started walking toward home. At a signal from Sharon, the rest of the family followed. Though discussion was needed, Sharon wasn't sure whether it should be between just herself and Michael or should include all of her children.

The spurt of energy Dee Dee had displayed proved short-lived. She yawned and sleepily rubbed her eyes. She was sound asleep on Michael's shoulders by the time they reached home.

Sharon quickly excluded her from a family talk. Whispering so as not to wake her, Sharon directed Michael to hand his sister over to Merry. She instructed Merry to carry Dee Dee upstairs and put her into bed after washing at least one layer of dirt off her hands and face.

Hoping she was reading everyone's expressions correctly, Sharon decided against a family meeting. Merry, Tim and Theresa seemed totally untroubled by Michael's remarks, but her eldest's usually sunny countenance was still dark and brooding. It was Michael whom she needed to talk to and Michael who needed to talk. She would get far more out of him if she got him alone.

Manufacturing an excuse to make a trip to a small grocery store—famous as the only store in town open until midnight—Sharon conned Michael into accompanying her. They drove toward their destination in silence until Michael suddenly said, "Okay, Mom, I'm on to you. You don't really need a gallon of milk when there's already two fresh ones in the refrigerator. You wanna know what's eating me . . . right?"

Sharon chuckled with relief, thankful that her two blond children had inherited at least one thing from her. Both Merry and Michael had quick tempers but cooled off quickly. Theirs was a perfect counterbalance to the brooding temperaments passed down to Tim and Theresa from their father. Dee Dee? She was obviously a throwback to a previous generation.

"You're on to me," Sharon confessed. "Would you like to go somewhere for a Coke and talk about it?"

Realizing any local place would be full of Michael's friends, they drove to a diner at the outskirts of the next town. Sitting across a Formica-topped table from Michael, Sharon shook off a feeling of déjà vu; but the brawny young man across from her was her son, not his father twenty years before. Though father and son were remarkably similar in coloring and physical features, Michael was his own unique person.

"Are you in love with Sam?" Michael asked bluntly as soon as they'd been served. The conversation during the last part of the twenty-minute drive had centered on football practice, Michael's new friends, adjustments to a small town and living with Aunt Di. To Sharon's overwhelming relief, Michael was happy in all those new aspects of his life. However, until this moment, they'd avoided any mention of Sam.

Not sure of the wisdom of sharing her feelings toward Sam, Sharon responded with a question. "How would you feel if I were?"

Michael moved his arms from the top of the booth and rested his forearms on the table. He pulled the wrapper from his straw and wadded the small sleeve of paper into a tight ball between his thumb and forefinger.

Sharon held her breath, waiting tensely for Michael's response. He tossed the tiny white ball into the ashtray beneath the jukebox unit at their booth, and neatly evaded a direct answer. "Would it make any difference if I didn't like it?"

"Yes, Michael, it would," Sharon answered honestly, deciding they'd tiptoed around the main issue long enough. Recognizing she was handing her son a great deal of power, she nevertheless stated, "You know I would never do anything that would make you, your sisters or your brother unhappy."

Looking up, he faced her with a direct gaze, vividly blue and totally guileless. He let out his breath in a soft whistle. "That's pretty heavy, Mom. I mean, you're saying you'd put us kids before your own happiness?"

"That's what I'm saying," she confirmed, praying inwardly that she'd never have to make such a choice. "What exactly are you saying?"

"I don't know," he replied, confusion clouding his eyes. He shifted nervously on the bench. Sharon fought the urge to prompt him, but knew it would be best to wait. Michael may have looked like his father, but he was much better able to verbalize his feelings.

"I mean Sam's all right," he began hesitantly. "But . . . he's not Dad." He focused his attention on his drink, twirling the glass and watching the ice bobble in the dark liquid. "You're my mom and . . . and . . . It just seems weird to think of you and Sam...uh...it's none of my business, I guess."

"No, Michael, it's not really any of your business, but I can see it bothers you to think of Sam and I—" Sharon paused to search for the right words "—having a deeply personal relationship," she finished carefully. "I'm guessing that you feel like I'm being disloyal to your father. Sort of unfaithful?"

Michael brought his head up sharply. A half smile banished the furrows that had marred the smooth skin between his brows. He gave a sheepish shrug. "Kind of dumb, huh? I mean it's not like you're still married, exactly."

"It's not dumb, Michael," Sharon assured him. "I've wrestled with the same feelings. Remember this. No matter what happens between Sam and me or any other man, I loved your father very much. There will always be a special place in my heart for him that no one else will ever occupy. I haven't forgotten him, honey, and I never will. I fell in love with your father when I was younger than you are. The thirteen years of marriage I was lucky enough to have with him were happy ones."

Michael tossed the straw aside and guzzled his soda down in two long swallows. Wiping his mouth with the back of his hand, he grinned at her, and Sharon knew that she'd somehow found the right words. "Thanks, Mom, and . . . uh . . . I'm sorry."

"For what?"

"For being stupid."

"You're never stupid, Mike. Just a little mixed up sometimes, and that's okay. Everybody gets a little mixed up and confused now and then." She smiled at him and then drained the rest of her coffee.

"It's kinda hard being the man in the family. You gotta worry about everyone."

"Will you do me a favor, Mike?" Sharon asked gently. "Sure."

"Enjoy being sixteen and let me do the worrying about the family. You've always been there for me and your brother and sisters whenever the chips were down. That's all I or your father could ever ask of you."

Michael shot her a cocky grin, but Sharon could sense his relief. "I do all right."

"More than all right," she amended. "So . . . are you ready to go back home, now?"

He pushed his empty glass to the middle of the table. "Yep." He slid out of the booth and waited for her. When Sharon reached for the check, Michael grabbed it from her hands. "My treat, Mom," he told her, then sauntered over to the cashier and paid the check.

On the way out of the diner, he suddenly commented, "You called me Mike." His expression and tone registered surprise. In all his sixteen and a half years, his mother had always called him Michael, claiming it avoided confusion with his father.

"I guess I did," Sharon verified, as surprised as her son that she'd dropped the formality. "Do you mind?"

"Nope."

Sharon felt very pleased with herself and her son during their companionable ride back to the house. In future, she had to make sure the lines of communication always remained open between them. Then, no matter what happened, things would work out. She had known that Mike was well on his way to becoming a man, but as they walked arm in arm to the house, she had reason to believe he was even further along than she'd thought.

"One last thing, Mom," he stated bluntly. "You'd better make sure Sam isn't just after your bod."

"Michael!" Sharon couldn't prevent her incredulous squeak nor her slip back into using the name she'd always called him.

"I had to say it, Mom. I'm a guy, and I know how they think." He gazed down at her, his expression very adult and solemn. "Be careful, okay?"

"I'll be careful, Mike," she assured him, not knowing which she wanted to do more, laugh or cry. "And Mike?"

"Yeah."

"I'm sorry I jumped all over you tonight."

"It's okay." He dropped an arm around her shoulders and gave her a squeeze.

9

SHARON AND DIANA arrived a few minutes early to the monthly meeting of the Women's Heritage League. Aunt Di wanted her niece to meet some of the League's members before the evening's program commenced. As they approached a group of women clustered in the back of the library's public-meeting room, Sharon recognized only Lydia Krouse.

During Diana's introductions, Sharon got the uncomfortable impression that she'd already been the topic of conversation. The ladies were polite when they greeted her, but she sensed a reserve she couldn't account for until a few moments later, when Mrs. Krouse took hold of her arm and drew her aside.

In a hushed voice Lydia said, "Sharon, dear, after what I've heard here tonight, I feel it my duty to warn you. People are beginning to talk about you and Sam."

Sharon tried to appear composed. "What kind of talk, Mrs. Krouse?" she inquired.

The older woman leaned closer and whispered conspiratorially, "I'm sure you could clear this up immediately, but Ada Grant told me that you and Sam made quite a spectacle of yourselves at the youth center yesterday. Of course, I told her there was a perfectly logical explanation for such behavior. Since I, myself, have witnessed your growing affection for one another, I suspect we'll soon be hearing a wedding announcement. Isn't that true?"

Sharon stammered, taken aback. "Ah... well... ah..."

"No need to be embarrassed, dear," Lydia assured. "I told Ada that things were done differently now than in our day, but I was certain Sam would soon do the right thing by you. After all, you have those five lovely children to think about, and Sam's position in the community to consider."

Sharon felt sick in the pit of her stomach. Mrs. Krouse might just as well have said that she expected Sam to make an honest woman of her. If Mrs. Krouse felt that way, how many others did?

Sharon was saved from having to respond to Lydia's comments when the meeting was called to order. "We'll talk more later, dear," Mrs. Krouse said, then hurried away to rejoin her friends.

Sharon stumbled to the nearest empty place, wishing she could disappear into the flowered cushions of the love seat. She had to maintain her poise, even though she had never felt more shattered. People were talking. People were looking. She felt as if a scarlet letter had been burned into her forehead.

What was she going to do? She hated the answer, but knew it was the only choice she had. She must break off with Sam, and the sooner the better. Her greatest fear about what might happen if anyone suspected the depth of their involvement was coming to pass. She had to take action before those she loved most were hurt by vicious tongues. Up until this evening, she'd gone along with Sam and allowed herself to believe that their personal life was no one's business but their own. Now, she knew if they continued their affair, they would both pay a terrible price.

So caught up in her despair, Sharon didn't realize Sam had entered the room and taken his place behind the podium. He began to speak. At the sound of his voice, her whole body contracted, and her heart felt as if it were being squeezed in a vise. She loved Sam with every ounce of her being, but they had no future.

She didn't dare look at him, knowing her feelings for him would show in her eyes. Anyone watching would guess how deeply she felt. Since an announcement of their marriage wasn't pending, Sharon couldn't afford to add more fuel to the gossip already circulating. If she looked at Sam, even once, she'd be caught up in the spell of his wonderful gray eyes, feel the pull of his charisma on every sense she possessed.

Somehow, she was going to have to find the strength to break off with him. Time. She needed some time, a period of solitude to collect herself and prepare for what had to be done. If only she could escape the meeting. Instead she had to sit still, appearing no more or less attentive than the next person as she listened to the mayor's speech.

"Thanks to the gracious contributions of both time and money from people like yourselves," Sam enthused into the microphone, "the youth of our community will soon have a place to call their own. And what a community it will be. Owing to the foresight and planning of our hardworking city council, new industries have been attracted to our area to ensure the future prosperity of our town and assure that our youth will have jobs waiting for them when they finish their school years."

Sam finished his speech to the League with a rousing flourish, predicting a bright future for Rhodesboro. A strong round of applause followed during which he smiled and gave the thumbs-up signal, then sat down.

Sam faced the audience of approximately forty women, but his gaze was on only one—the chestnut-haired woman with the big brown eyes who was seated on one of the love seats along the edge of the room. No matter how hard he willed otherwise, she managed to avoid his eyes.

Hell, he hadn't thought the little argument they'd had yesterday had been that serious. Evidently he'd underestimated the strength of her feelings. As he listened with only part of his mind to the League's president sum up the evening, Sam contemplated Sharon Markovski and his feelings for her. Perhaps he'd underestimated those, too.

Fond? Fond seemed too mild a word and indicated an even milder emotion. Definitely not fond. His feelings for her were anything but mild. They bordered on obsessive. He wanted her now even more than he had that first day.

Even so, if he didn't want the whole world knowing what was on his mind, he'd be wise to look elsewhere. That off-the-shoulder sundress Sharon was wearing was driving him crazy. How easy it would be to slip it down to her waist, bare her beautiful breasts to his lips.

Sam cleared his throat and jammed his hands into his coat pockets. If he wasn't careful, he wouldn't be able to stand up without embarrassing himself and shocking the good ladies of Rhodesboro.

"Again, we of the Women's Heritage League want to thank our mayor, Sam Jefferson, for coming this evening." Inez Graham's remarks caught Sam's attention. Surely this was the end of the meeting. Another round of polite applause followed and Sam geared himself up to spring for his quarry. He nearly hooted with joy when Inez announced adjournment and encouraged everyone to partake of the cookies and punch waiting on a table at the back of the room.

"Sharon, good to see you here tonight," greeted Arlene Bennett with a friendly smile, having made her way to Sharon's side as soon as the meeting adjourned. "The League could use some new blood, don't you think, Diana?" she asked, including Sharon's aunt in her greeting, but not waiting for a reply.

"I hope you're going to join us," Arlene enthused. "Of course, we can't guarantee every meeting will be as interesting as the one we had tonight," she went on in the near nonstop way Sharon had come to realize was typical of Arlene. "Sam not only gives a good speech, but he's easy on the eyes, too."

"I quite agree on all counts," Diana said, a twinkle of humor in her blue eyes. "Just don't scare off this potential member here with talk that some of our meetings are boring. That's not the way to entice someone to join."

"Yipes, you're so right," Arlene agreed with a small giggle. She caught Sharon's arm and guided her toward the refreshment table. "Actually, the League is quite fun, if you're into history, and your aunt already let it out that you are."

"I suppose I'm caught then," Sharon said, knowing she was caught in more ways than one. She'd hoped to escape the meeting quickly, put off talking to Sam a while longer, but there was no way she could rush off without appearing rude. In a matter of minutes, she was going to have to face him and the inevitable. No matter how badly she loved him, wanted him, they couldn't go on as they were. He would have to accept that.

The flutters in her stomach escalated into back flips as she anticipated their upcoming confrontation. While she mingled with the other women, she was constantly on the alert for Sam's approach, but he didn't come near her. As the group began to thin out and it looked as if she would be able to leave any minute, Sharon's anxieties did an about-face. After gearing herself up for their meeting, convincing herself it was for the best, it was beginning to look as if the agony might have to be postponed to another night.

Sam was making no effort to seek her out. He was spending his time wooing votes for re-election. From the comments she'd overheard, the consensus was that Sam was a shoo-in for another term in office.

How could he lose? He had a smile that would dazzle anyone who wasn't blind. A face with near-perfect features. A voice that could charm a listener into believing anything he had to say.

Looks aside, votes cast for Sam would be fully justified. No matter what he thought, Samuel Adams Jefferson lived up to his exalted name. He was a man of conviction and integrity. He had great energy and passion.

Passion? Oh yes, Sharon had firsthand knowledge of the kind of passion Sam was capable of. Unlike the other women in the room, she also had hands-on information about the magnificent body hidden beneath his crisp tan linen sport coat, shirt, tie and cream-colored dress pants. She knew what he looked like in those rapturous moments, just before he . . .

Suddenly Sharon couldn't stand it any longer. The room was far too warm. Luckily, she was at the edge of a group of women and could place her punch cup down on a table to make her escape without anyone's being the wiser. She nodded to her aunt as she passed, mumbling something about getting some air.

Sharon stepped outside, welcoming the cooler, fresher air on her skin and into her lungs. She walked a few feet away from the building. The voices from inside could still be heard, but seemed far away. Once, she thought she heard Sam's deep rumbling laugh, and even at this distance, she felt a familiar tingle run down her spine. Tears gathered in her eyes when she thought about doing without that feeling for the rest of her life.

She leaned against one of the ancient elms that had survived the Dutch elm disease that had wiped out most of the species across the state. Its rough bark rasped against her bare arm, but she welcomed the stability its thick trunk provided. This tree was a survivor and, whatever happened, she would be, too.

Footsteps sounded behind her and Sharon turned. It was Sam.

"Diana suggested I drive you home," he said, coming to a stop in front of her. "She got caught up in some discussion with Inez Graham, and said she'd be along later."

Sharon gazed into his eyes for several seconds, then nodded. "I need to talk to you, Sam."

"Sharon, if there's something wrong—"

"Not here." Sharon stepped away from the tree. "Let's go back to your place."

"Okay," he returned brusquely as he took her arm. After handing her into the car, Sam slid behind the wheel and jammed the key into the ignition. He felt extremely uneasy; his fingers were shaking. "Are we going to talk about that argument we had yesterday, or is something else bothering you?"

"What happened yesterday is only part of it, Sam," Sharon said, her voice almost breaking over his name.

"I see." Sam pulled out onto the street. He asked no further questions. He was too scared. The sight of those beautiful soft eyes of hers swimming in tears terrified him. Something had happened since he'd last seen her, something that had hurt her far more than their little skirmish at the center.

She was going to break off with him; he knew it. And he couldn't let it happen. He loved her. He wasn't just deeply fond of her, passionately attracted and intimately involved. He loved her.

ONCE INSIDE the carriage house, Sharon sat on the couch to wait while Sam made coffee. Looking around her, she marveled at the transformation that had taken place in the carriage house over such a short time. The main room was completed except for the bookcases Sam planned to install on each side of the fireplace.

Oriental rugs defined the living and dining areas— bright patches of color against the pegged oak floor. Furniture, some of it antique pieces his parents had had the foresight to remove from the old Jefferson house not long before the fire, had been brought out of storage and artfully interspersed with more modern pieces in a tasteful eclectic mix.

She knew that up in the loft, only a small section of subflooring between the bed and the bathroom waited for a layer of oak. In a matter of days, that would be finished, too. Considering that Sam had undertaken the entire renovation himself with only the knowledge gained in "do it yourself" books, it was truly amazing.

His workshop supplies and remaining lumber had been relegated to the garage the previous week. "I'm tired of living in the middle of a construction site, and all the rough work's done," Sam had said when he'd come over to the main house to request some assistance from the boys. "In another few weeks, I'm going to have everything just the way I want it."

The perfect home for a confirmed bachelor, Sharon decided miserably, that's what he wanted. One bedroom, one bath, a small, efficient kitchen. He had made the carriage house into a model living space for the single man.

Sam placed two mugs of coffee on the table, but Sharon didn't seem to notice. She was so deeply in thought, she didn't even move when he sat down beside her. He looked into her wounded eyes, and the breath went out of him. He took her hand. "Tell me what's wrong, Sharon."

Sharon stared down at the hand holding hers, then into the eyes of the man who held her heart. "I got cornered by Lydia Krouse this morning. People know about us, Sam."

A muscle jerked in his jaw. "What did she say to you?"

Sharon sighed. "You know what she said, what everyone is going to be saying if we go on like this. We're having an affair, and that's big news in a small town, even bigger news when it involves the mayor."

Instead of arguing the point, as she'd expected, Sam nodded. He looked angry, but his tone conveyed nothing of the rage that shone in his eyes. "So what do you propose we do about it?"

Mustering her reserve of courage, she decided to go for broke. "I love you, Sam, but if you don't feel the same way then it's over."

The rage in his eyes disappeared. "Say that again," he ordered huskily, his relief so strong it was difficult for him to speak.

"I love you," she repeated simply and quietly.

Sam carried her fingers to his lips. His eyes were soft, dark and velvety as he kissed her palm. Looking into those eyes, Sharon felt a spark of hope. Was it possible! Did Sam love her just as much as she loved him? Did he want them to stay together as badly as she did?

Sam drew her onto his lap and cradled her tenderly against him. "My sweet, Sharon. You don't know what hearing you say that has done for me." He drew in a shuddering breath, then adjusted her in his arms. This was where she belonged. His Sharon. Bending his head, he kissed the woman he loved.

It was a kiss so tender yet so intense it sent a message to Sharon's soul. This man was her mate—the opposite part of her that made her complete. She wound both arms around Sam's neck and pressed herself closer and closer. She loved him; oh how she loved him. Though she couldn't speak, every heartbeat should tell him so, just as his throbbing pulse was telling her.

When he finally lifted his lips from hers, Sharon sighed in blissful satisfaction, but Sam had only begun to tell her how he felt. "I love having you around, Sharon. I love the sound of your voice, the color of your eyes. I love hearing you talk about your day and telling you about mine. I love knowing someone cares about me and how I feel. In short, my lovely short person, I love everything about you—very much."

Sharon nestled herself against his shoulder and lifted her head so she could see his face. When they were long married, when the mundane sometimes overshadowed the sublime, she would remember this perfect moment and be renewed. "I love everything about you, too, Sam. I love the way you listen when I babble on and on. I love the sensitivity and caring you've shown me and my children and my aunt. I love listening to your dreams about the future of this town. I love your eyes, your laugh, your gorgeous body. I just plain old-fashioned love you."

"Sweetheart." Sam's smile matched the joy he saw in her eyes. "I'd say we've got a pretty good thing going here, no matter what some old busybody says."

"Mmm," Sharon murmured. "I couldn't agree more."

Sam kissed her again, then muttered thickly. "Lord, how I need you. I was so afraid I was losing you."

"You'll never lose me, Sam. I need you, too, so much."

Sam scooped her up and strode toward the stairs. As soon as they reached the loft, they came together with barely restrained eagerness, celebrating the love they'd just declared. Their fingers trembled as they rid themselves of their clothing. They fell upon the bed, naked and vulnerable, both needing to give as much as to receive.

The open admission of their feelings brought something new to their lovemaking. Sharon had never felt more bold, more anxious to touch and to feel, more willing to give all of herself. She worshiped Sam's body with her mouth, her hands, her eyes and was awed by the suppressed power she saw and felt in every corded muscle, every tendon and bone. Beneath her touch, he was helpless, submitting to her as easily as she always submitted to him.

When he could stand it no longer, Sam returned her loving fully, restraining himself until he'd tasted every inch of her. His touch had never been more worshipful, more adoring. He whispered his love for her over and over again as he caressed her, kissed his way down her body.

At last, they joined in tune with each other as never before. In loving, they were truly one, for tonight they arrived at every new plane along the way toward fulfillment with an intensity neither had ever felt. Sharon strained against Sam, pressing her cheek into his chest as the tremors came, subsided slightly, then returned in stronger and stronger waves. She could hear the beating of his heart, a frantic pounding that accompanied the waves of pleasure and was echoed by her own frenzied pulse.

"Sharon . . . oh, my sweet . . ." The words were a plea and a tormented cry as Sam yielded all of himself to the final savage swell that overtook him. He stiffened and shuddered, holding himself deep inside her as she weathered an equal storm.

Afterward they lay locked together, unmoving, until the rushing sound of their breathing evened and slowed. Neither was willing to give up the soothing feel of the other's skin, and they remained joined in that position for long minutes. Eventually Sam rolled her atop him, then held her gently stroking the indentation of her spine.

"Did I mention how much I love your body?" Sharon spoke against the base of his neck, pressing her lips to his warm flesh. "If so, it bears repeating."

Sam smoothed his palms over her buttocks. "Madam, you may repeat those words as often as you like, as long as I am free to do the same. I could spend hours elaborating on the subject of your body. I don't know why I avoided mention of the word love. Loving you is easy."

"I'm so glad, Sam." Sharon slid off his body and curled up next to him, resting her head on his shoulder. "I was so afraid love and marriage didn't appeal to you."

Sam hesitated a fraction too long before answering. "I find loving you very appealing."

Sharon lifted her head off his shoulder, then sat up, drawing the bed sheet over her breasts. Praying he would calm her sudden fear, she asked quietly, "But marriage, Sam? Does that appeal to you?"

Without speaking, Sam sat up beside her. He positioned the pillows behind him, then leaned back and stared up at the ceiling. Voice strained, he shattered her dreams with his own question. "Can't we take this one step at a time?"

Sharon closed her eyes. A cold hand twisted her insides. "I've always thought the step after loving was marriage."

"For you, maybe," Sam countered heavily. "But loving is new to me. I'm not as experienced at it as you are."

"No," Sharon agreed, her stomach tightening into a knot. "I suppose you're not, but then I'm not very experienced at loving without some commitment." Sharon rolled away from him, reaching for her clothes.

"Sharon, I do love you."

"And I love you." She continued dressing, unable to look at him for fear she wouldn't be able to leave him if she did. "Where do we go from here?" She spoke quietly, inwardly flailing herself for naively assuming that marriage would follow their declarations of love.

"Sharon...I...I need some time." Following her lead, Sam hauled himself out of bed and started pulling on his pants.

Sharon felt as if her clothing was all that was keeping her together. It hurt so much to know she'd been fooling herself from the beginning. Sam had told her straight out that all he offered was an affair. "How much time do you need, Sam? Days? Weeks? Years?"

Sam struggled to hide his frustration. It would be so easy to reaffirm his love for her and set a wedding date. If that was all there was to it, he'd be on his knees in front of her in a minute. However, there were five children involved here. Couldn't she see that he was trying to put them ahead of his own happiness?

"Sharon. I'm not sure marriage between us would be right. I don't know if I can give you what you need." Sam began pacing. "Those wonderful kids of yours need a father, and you need a partner in raising them. I'm just not sure I'm capable of that role. The last thing I'd ever want to do is mess them up."

Sharon's knees threatened to give way, and she sank down on the bed. "You've been great with my kids. They love you." She could understand Sam's anxiety, but not why he couldn't see what a good father he would make. "Parenting is always a gamble. Nobody goes into it knowing they're going to be good at it. You just do the best you can."

"That's what I'm saying. I'm not ready to take that risk. I just don't know if my best is good enough, and I refuse to gamble with your children's emotional well-being." Sam wished he could take her in his arms and comfort her, but knew that would only make matters worse. He could sense her pulling away, and blurted in desperation, "I've told you all along that I don't see myself as a father, but that doesn't mean we have to give up what we have."

"Yes it does. You were right! I can't handle an affair. If anything would harm my children, our going on as we are would." Wrapping her arms around herself, Sharon held back a sob. She was determined not to cry, not now, not until later.

She felt as desolate as she had when Mike had died. This was perhaps worse, for Sam was still very much alive and she would feel the pain of losing him each time she saw him. Living so close, that would be often.

Sam couldn't refute what she'd said to him. Something infinitely precious was slipping through his fingers, and there was nothing he could do about it. If their affair continued, they risked a scandal that would hurt the children. If, feeling so unsure, he married her, he would hurt them even more.

Yet, how could he let her go? She was the only woman he wanted. The only one he'd felt enough for to hurt over. If love was enough, and there was only the two of them to consider, he'd get down on his knees and beg her to marry him. He cursed himself for not being the man she needed, not being strong enough to take on the whole Markovski package. If he couldn't be a father to her kids, he didn't deserve her.

Perhaps he was selfish, but he had to hold her one more time, if only to say goodbye. He moved around the bed, intending to enclose her in his arms, but Sharon stopped him.

"No." She held up her hands defensively. "Don't touch me. Please."

"I'm so sorry for hurting you, Sharon," Sam uttered brokenly, every muscle tensed at the finality in her tone. "I hate the thought of losing you."

"I know," Sharon whispered, sadness overwhelming her.

Sam's mouth tightened even more, his eyes filled with emotion. "Please don't hate me."

"I don't hate you, Sam." Sharon stood up and walked slowly toward the stairs. "I'm just very sorry for both of us."

Sam watched her go. "So am I," he rasped in a heart-sick tone. "God knows, I've never been more sorry in my life."

10

SOCIOLOGY, PSYCHOLOGY, HISTORY. None of them held Sharon's attention, and she gave up all pretext of studying. With one ear tuned to every sound in the house, her powers of concentration were nil. She glanced at her watch—2:00 A.M.

Turning off the light on the study table, she rose from her chair. With a little luck, she might still be able to get a few hours' sleep. Dee Dee had come down with a virus, and though her nausea had subsided, her temperature was still above normal and she had a terrible cough.

Sharon went down the hall and checked on her youngest once more. Dee Dee was sleeping peacefully, though her forehead was still a bit warm. She was probably over the worst of it, but Merry and Tim had shown signs earlier this evening of contracting the same illness. Neither had had much appetite, and their eyes had been a little too bright.

Standing in the hallway at the base of the third-floor steps, Sharon listened for the boys. It was quiet. Maybe she'd been imagining symptoms. A stop in the older girls' room showed they were both sleeping, but Merry seemed fitful.

Sighing, Sharon went back to her bedroom, unable to dismiss a feeling of dread. It was entirely possible that the household was about to come under a siege of the flu. Restless, she moved to the window and stared through the darkness. Beyond the bare branches of the sycamore tree, a light shone from the carriage house. Sam was still awake. She wondered if he was thinking about her. If she haunted his dreams the way he haunted hers.

In but a handful of weeks, the friendship, the support and the loving she'd shared with Sam had become an essential part of her life. He had filled a void she hadn't admitted existed, one she doubted would ever be filled again.

It was almost November, nearly two months since she and Sam had broken up, but she still dreamed about him practically every night. No matter what she told herself, her subconscious reached out for him, refusing to accept that what they'd had was over. In her dreams, he came to her, loving her and making love to her, confident in his ability to be a father figure for her children.

By day, however, she'd had to look at things far more realistically. As much as Sam might profess to love her, it wasn't enough. She came with responsibilities that he wasn't willing to take on. Fantasizing about a day when he would change his mind was just that. A fantasy.

Over the past few weeks, the children had reported that they'd often seen Sam walking in the woods. Theresa had come upon him at "thinking rock" on numerous occasions. Sharon had hoped he had spent his time reevaluating his position. But, with each day that passed, her hopes had died a little more.

Their insecurities would always keep them apart. She couldn't bear the censure she and her family would face if she and Sam remained lovers. And Sam was unwilling to believe he was capable of being a good parent. Maybe they were both fools. Certainly both would suffer for it.

Aunt Di had sensed Sharon's pain early on, but other than saying she was sorry it hadn't worked out between them, the woman had held her own counsel. Lydia Krouse had called to confirm that Sharon and Sam were no longer seeing each other and assured her that all talk would die down now that she had come to her senses. Sharon had quietly hung up on the woman.

Initially the children hadn't been sensitive to their mother's feelings. They had bluntly asked her why she wasn't going out with Sam anymore. Nothing would have been more cruel than to tell them that she and Sam had broken up because he didn't think himself capable of being their stepfather. Therefore she had lied and told them that she and Sam had simply decided they were incompatible, that they would always be good friends but nothing more. She knew her older children weren't quite buying that story, but, like Aunt Di, they hadn't pressed Sharon any further.

Leaning her forehead against the cold windowpane, Sharon damned the fates that had thrown Sam Jefferson into her life. She had to find a way to let go of her feelings for him. Whenever she saw him, she turned into a mass of quivering nerves. It was so hard to look at him without wanting him. Speak to him without recalling other, intimate, conversations.

She remembered their latest confrontation a few days back. She'd been folding laundry in the kitchen when she'd heard a screech of brakes and then the sickening crunch of metal against metal. A child's wail of terror had followed the ominous noise.

Heart in her throat, Sharon had thrown open the door. Screaming Dee Dee's name, she'd dashed down the porch steps and into the driveway.

"She's okay," Sam shouted, already on his knees in front of the sobbing little girl. "I hit her bike. She wasn't on it."

"Oh, thank heavens." Sharon sagged with relief. A split-second inventory confirmed Sam's statement. The child was only frightened, not hurt. Of the two of them, Sam looked much worse.

His skin was ashen, his face lined with concern. His hands were shaking as he stroked Dee Dee's hair. His tone was unsteady when he said, "Thank God, it was only the trike. I heard that crunch and then her crying.... I don't think I've ever moved so fast in my life."

"My tricycle's all broked, Mommy," Dee Dee whimpered, running to her mother for comfort. "I didn't mean to leave it in the driveway."

Sharon lifted her daughter into her arms and hugged her tightly. "It's okay, honey. I'm so glad you're all right."

Over Dee Dee's head, Sharon gazed at Sam. He looked as if he'd committed a far worse crime than driving over a hand-me-down tricycle. Sharon could well imagine how frightened he'd been when it happened. He looked as much in need of comfort as Dee Dee, and she yearned to take him in her arms. Two months ago she would have.

"It's not your fault her trike was in the driveway," she said, the gentle words the only thing she could offer to ease his guilt.

Obviously still shaken by thoughts of how close he'd come to hitting her child, Sam repeated his regret. "I feel terrible about this. Will you let me replace the bike?"

"Will you, Mommy?" Dee Dee piped up, her tears miraculously evaporating.

"We'll talk about this later, Dee Dee," Sharon replied noncommittally. Putting the child down, she took her hand, preparing to lead her into the house.

"But I don't want to talk later," Dee Dee argued. "I want a new bike, now!"

"Dee Dee!" Sharon spoke sharply, effectively silencing her. "That will be enough."

Dee Dee's lower lip trembled, and she dug her chin into her chest. The tassel at the top of her hat quivered as she whined, "But Mommy..."

"You go into the house and up to your room, Dee Dee. I'll be in to talk to you in a few minutes," Sharon said firmly. She couldn't help but smile as the child turned away, dragging her small feet every step of the way up the back-porch stairs.

"Weren't you a little hard on her?" Sam suggested, as soon as Dee Dee disappeared into the house. "The poor thing is heartbroken over her bike."

"She'll recover," Sharon assured him. Suddenly aware that she was standing outside in her shirt sleeves, the frost-edged October wind raising gooseflesh on her arms, she was anxious to return to the warmth of the kitchen. Not only that, but talking with Sam was always difficult, and the quicker she was done with it the better.

"Dee Dee hated that tricycle. She's been begging for a two-wheeler for months," she explained. "When she heard that offer of yours, she jumped at the chance of getting one. Before that happens, she's going to have to learn to be a bit more responsible."

That said, she started for the house.

"I do owe her one," Sam maintained staunchly, his gloved hands closing over Sharon's shoulders. Turning her toward him, he said, "After all, I should have been more careful; I just assumed the driveway was clear. I need to do something to salve my guilty conscience."

Sharon shivered. After all this time, his touch still tortured her with images of what might have been. Everything in her longed for him. She had to get away before she surrendered to her feelings and threw herself into his arms.

"I'm sorry, but no new bike," she insisted, biting off his words. "I told you right after we moved in that I considered it the children's responsibility to keep their toys out of the driveway. Dee Dee has to learn the consequences of breaking the rules."

Noticing her trembling, Sam rubbed his hands up and down her arms. He was glad of any excuse to touch her. He only wished he could haul her against him and kiss away all of her fears and his own. Unfortunately, he couldn't do that. Until he was absolutely certain he could give her all she needed, he had to leave things as they were. "Okay, I guess you know best," he said with resignation.

Sharon nodded and tried to step away, but his fingers closed over her upper arm. "Sharon, I . . ."

Startled by the catch in his voice, Sharon looked into his eyes. The emotion she saw there stunned her. His invitation was still open. He wanted her, maybe still loved her, and it was as hard for him to keep his distance as it was for her. She read something else in those shadowy gray eyes. He was still unprepared to offer anything more than he had before. She couldn't put herself through that again. Sharon pulled back and this time he let her go. "I . . . I'd better get inside."

"I could use a cup of coffee," Sam challenged softly.

"I don't think that would be a good idea," Sharon returned, backing farther away.

"Are you afraid to spend time with me—alone?"

Sharon sucked in her breath. "I'm not afraid to be alone with you," she vowed, but couldn't meet his eyes.

She was lying. She was afraid. Even in the unromantic setting of her kitchen, she would find it impossible not to think about resuming where they'd left off.

"Prove it."

Sharon's chin shot up, and her eyes locked with his. Maybe it was time to test herself. Until today, they'd gone through the motions of being only friendly acquaintances. Maybe it was time to prove that was all they truly were or ever would be. "All right. It is a cold day, and I could do with a cup of coffee myself."

Once inside her kitchen, Sharon kept her eyes on the coffeepot she'd set on the stove, but her thoughts were on the man seated at the table. She heard the rustle of his overcoat, knew when he draped it over the counter and when he lowered his long, lean body into a chair.

Now that they were inside, an awkward silence stretched out between them. Nothing was said until Sharon placed two steaming mugs down on the table. "Black with one teaspoon of sugar," she recalled as she pulled out the chair across from him and sat down.

"I remember a lot of things about you, too," he remarked smoothly.

Sharon's hand jerked. A few drops of coffee splashed over the edge of her mug. Nervously she dabbed at the small puddle on the tablecloth with a napkin. "Are you deliberately trying to make this difficult?"

His gray eyes seemed electric as they burned into hers. He took a long swallow of his coffee, watching her over the rim. When finally he spoke, his voice was a mixture of gravel and silk, a tone she'd never heard. "I didn't know what hard was until you walked out of my life. I miss you, Sharon. I don't know how much longer I can handle missing you."

Sharon could feel the tears on her cheeks, but was too frozen in anguish to brush them away. "Has anything changed?" she choked out.

"Only that I love you even more." His voice was quiet, strained, sad.

He left her sitting there, then, tears streaming from her eyes. She heard the door open and close. And he was gone.

SHARON TURNED AWAY from the window. She had to stop dwelling on something she couldn't change. She got into bed, switched off the remaining light and closed her eyes. Willing herself to relax, she finally fell asleep.

An hour later she was awakened by an acute attack of nausea. She barely made it to the bathroom in time. She was still draped over the toilet bowl when she heard rapid footsteps in the bathroom directly overhead. The unmistakable sounds of someone losing the contents of his stomach followed.

"Oh Lord!" Sharon exclaimed weakly, as she rose to her feet. "It's an epidemic." She'd always counted herself lucky that, somehow, she and the children had been sick simultaneously only once. That fiasco had been years ago before Dee Dee had been born and Sharon, fortunately, had suffered only a mild case of the virus that had run through the family.

As the cold clammy feel of her skin was replaced by chills, Sharon recognized the first symptoms of a rising fever. Shakily, she leaned against the vanity. Wiping her face, she wondered if she could possibly have enough strength to climb to the third floor and check on the boys.

"You can do it," she told herself. She left the bathroom and started toward the steps leading to the third floor, chanting, "One of the boys needs you," under her breath. Grasping the banister, she placed one foot on the first step.

She tried to ignore the beginning wave of another attack. Gulping and swallowing fast, she gripped the banister with both hands. Calling upon the optimistic philosophy of *The Little Engine That Could*, she started to mount the stairs again. She'd made it to the third step when she heard a bedroom door open. White-faced, her hand clamped over her mouth, Merry raced toward the bathroom.

"Oh, no," Sharon moaned, and sat down on the step. Down through the stairwell echoed the sound of the toilet flushing, water running in the sink, then another set of stumbling footsteps as brother joined brother in the small bathroom on the third floor.

Sharon's second attack was becoming too persistent to ignore, and mother joined daughter. Together they weathered a storm of roiling waves of nausea.

Sharon managed to get Merry settled in bed, then stumbled back to her own. Teeth chattering, she wrapped herself in her old flannel robe and curled up beneath the blankets. Miserable, she gave up on the idea of helping any of her children. Her last thought before she succumbed to a hallucinatory stupor was that they were young adults and would just have to fend for themselves.

IN T-SHIRT AND JEANS, Sam sat in his kitchen. Taking sips of coffee, he skimmed the pages of the book lying open on the small oak table. It was going on nine in the morning, but he had given himself the day off and intended to spend the time boning up on a foreign subject.

As he reviewed the chapter index, Sam felt more and more overwhelmed. Dr. Spock had written over six hundred pages on subjects Sam had never thought about in his life. "Formula equipment," he read out loud. "Crying in the early weeks."

"There's a whole chapter here on thumb sucking!"

Sam continued flipping pages in the table of contents, his relief growing as he realized the wealth of information he might never have to digest. Unless the situation changed, he had no need to know about breast-feeding, the proper equipment for an infant layette or any other information contained in the 360 pages before he found the heading "Children, Ages Three through Six."

If it became necessary, he'd have months to study the first half of the book at a later date. For now, he needed to concentrate on the existing ages of the children he hoped to adopt.

He was heartened by the first sentence in the chapter on four-year-olds that basically said children in this stage of development felt that their parents were wonderful people. They wanted to be like them, talk like them and do what they do. According to Spock, the hostility period had pretty much run its course by this age. Of course, then there was another difficult stage, but he thought he could handle that one. Dee Dee was downright obnoxious at times and he'd been able to cope so far.

"Good thing," Sam muttered. "With everything else I might have to handle, I don't need Dee Dee going hostile on me."

A half hour later, Sam was again feeling depressed and totally inadequate. There was no way on earth he was going to be able to take on five children of various ages when he couldn't even understand the infinite complexities he'd just read concerning the average four-year-old. The section on imaginary worries and fears, alone, had been mind-boggling.

Dee Dee might call upon him to help handle her fear of death, the dark, dogs, fire engines or monsters. And each fear had to be dealt with in a different way. If he didn't memorize the entire chapter, he might botch the whole thing and do permanent damage to Dee Dee's emotional well-being.

"The hell with it!" Sam swore and tossed the book on the floor. "I'll never get the hang of all this."

When he'd told Sharon that she deserved a better father for her children than he could be, he'd meant it. But by God, if he'd come to realize nothing else in the past two months, he knew that no one could love them better than he did. Wasn't that enough to start with? Surely he could learn the basics of good parenting if he really set his mind to it. When all was said and done, he had no other choice. He loved them all, needed them desperately and somehow he was going to prove he was good enough for them.

Buying a copy of Spock's famous *Baby and Child Care* had seemed like a good way to begin. The bookstore had a whole section of child-rearing books, but he'd settled on the only one he'd ever heard of, figuring a book that had been reprinted nearly two hundred times must have something going for it.

In one short volume, he thought he'd find all he'd ever need to know about the care and feeding of children from birth to puberty. Upon reading it, he'd expected to feel more competent to assume the role of stepfather. Until a few minutes ago, he'd thought his solution to the problem of his ignorance had been logical.

He firmly believed that the first step in solving a problem was to recognize that there was one. He'd done that. He knew nothing about how to raise kids, but he sure knew something about how not to.

Unlike the way he'd been reared, he'd give his kids plenty of love and attention. Except those months when he and his father had restored that old Cadillac, he'd seen very little of the man. During the years prior to that isolated time, those important developmental years, Sam's father had spent nearly every waking hour concentrating on building his career.

His mother had been there a little more often, but she had been involved in so many community activities Sam had spent most of his childhood with only the housekeeper as company. He might not have been brought up with a positive example of parenting, but one could learn just as much from negative examples. He knew exactly what not to do. That had to be a step in the right direction.

Another was realizing he wouldn't be alone. Sharon was an excellent parent. He'd try to follow her example . . . or keep his big mouth shut. At least he'd had the good sense to do that the other day over the bicycle incident. No matter how much he had wanted to give Dee Dee a new bike, Sharon had been right. Accepting responsibility was an important lesson to learn at any age.

He was a grown man, but he'd not learned it until recently. He had a feeling it was much harder to deal with at thirty-eight than at four. He'd shunned his responsibilities, paid the price, but was now determined to become the father the Markovski children deserved. Besides, they were already his kids. No matter how many times he denied it, that was the truth of the matter.

He wasn't sure when he'd come to that awesome realization. It hadn't happened overnight. Maybe it had started with the strong swell of pride he'd felt when Mike scored a touchdown during the opening game of the season. Or maybe it had been when Theresa received the citizenship award for the paper she'd written on what it meant to be an American. When Merry had made the eighth-grade cheerleading squad. The time Tim had "shadowed" him for career day.

Or perhaps it had come home to him the day he'd run over Dee Dee's bike and felt a fear he'd never experienced before in his life. That little girl meant the world to him, and the thought of losing her had wrenched at his guts in much the same way as when he thought of losing her mother. They were both a part of him. All of them were a part of him, and he couldn't ignore his responsibilities any longer.

Sitting all alone in his newly renovated house, he felt empty. He had achieved everything he'd come to Rhodesboro to attain, but without Sharon and the kids he was miserable. He enjoyed his position as mayor and had developed a thriving law practice. He had the respect and admiration of the townspeople, but he'd never be satisfied until he had regained the respect and admiration of the woman he loved.

Sharon hadn't said it, but he knew he'd let her down terribly. He'd betrayed her trust in the most painful way possible. He'd become involved with her, become an integral part of her family, but when he'd been asked to make a commitment, he'd stepped back.

"You were an irresponsible coward!" he castigated himself aloud.

At the time he'd thought he'd been making a noble gesture, an unselfish decision for the good of Sharon and her children. He'd told himself that he'd screwed up his priorities for the first thirty-five years of his life and couldn't take the chance that he'd mess up someone else's. Hell, he'd been kidding himself. He wasn't noble or unselfish; he was just plain scared.

It had taken him two months to overcome his fear, but he'd done it. He'd had enough of the alternative. Silence and loneliness. Since he'd stopped seeing Sharon, the children's visits had gradually tapered off.

Sam reached over to the radio and flipped it on. He certainly needed some noise other than the sound of the mantel clock chiming over the fireplace. The chiming persisted, and Sam realized the sound wasn't the clock but the doorbell. A steady rap of knuckles against wood began to accompany the melodic chimes.

No doubt Lydia Krouse was at the door, hoping he'd rescue her cat. Sam welcomed her visit. The woman was going to get a good piece of his mind. Her vicious tongue had hurt Sharon, but he was going to make sure it never did again.

With grim determination, he got up from the table and headed for the door. By the way the woman was pounding, her damned cat must have climbed all the way to the top of her oak tree. Old Boris could take a flying leap as far as Sam was concerned.

He yanked open the door. "Okay, lady...! Theresa?" Sam stared openmouthed at the miniature of Sharon Markovski who stood shivering on his front step.

"You have to come, Sam. I can't do it by myself. You have to help me."

"Of course I'll help you, honey." Sam drew the obviously distraught little girl into the house. It was only forty degrees outside, and Theresa wasn't even wearing a jacket. Her nose was red from the cold and she was shivering.

Something was definitely wrong. Sharon would never allow one of her kids outside in the cold without a coat. Besides it was Friday, a weekday. Why wasn't Theresa in school?

"Everybody's sick," Theresa announced in panic, taking hold of Sam's hand and trying to drag him out the door. Tears began streaming from her large brown eyes, and her shoulders began to shake as she cried, "I don't know what to do."

Sam grabbed his jacket and tucked her inside it. He gave an uncertain glance at the book lying open on the table, then squared his shoulders. "That's all right, sweetheart. I do."

11

LET ME DIE, Sharon prayed silently, as the muscle spasms continued to rack her sore, empty stomach and her head throbbed with pain. If she lay perfectly still, the spasms didn't require another fruitless journey to the bathroom. She was determined to remain immobile, for there was no vacancy in that room. During the night, one by one, the rest of the family had dropped like flies. Only Theresa hadn't succumbed to the flu that had struck the household with a vengeance.

Sharon felt a cool cloth being placed on her forehead. "Bless you, honey, but go help somebody else. I'm fine."

"You don't look fine."

Sharon moaned. She was even sicker than she thought, obviously hallucinating. She could swear Theresa's voice had dropped to a baritone.

"Can you sip a little of this?"

A straw was inserted gently between Sharon's dry lips. Dutifully, she complied, no longer caring that her mind had conjured up Sam to be her nurse. A more unlikely candidate for the job she couldn't imagine, but obviously, her subconscious had no sense. At least in her hallucination, Sam knew what to do. The citrus-flavored drink was exactly what her dehydrated body craved, and it seemed to settle her stomach.

"Mommy, Mommy," called a weak little voice.

Instinctively Sharon started to rise, but a heavy hand pushed her down on the mattress. "You're not going anywhere, sweetheart. I'll take care of Dee Dee."

Tired of this particular delusion, Sharon opened one eye. As soon as she saw who was bending over her, the other eye flew open. "Sam! What are you doing here?"

"Emptying buckets, doing laundry, changing beds and forcing fluids," he answered calmly. "I called the doctor, and he said this nasty stuff is going around. It just has to run its course. Can you think of anything else I can do to help?"

In her present condition Sharon would have welcomed assistance from the devil himself. Too weak to question further, she muttered, "You're doing fine." Her eyes fluttered closed for a moment, then quickly reopened. "Aunt Di! How is she?"

"Better than you," Sam assured as he left to answer Dee Dee's call. "Rest now, Sharon. You don't need to worry about anyone. I'm here."

In the pink-and-white bedroom down the hall, Sam rocked Dee Dee on his lap until she fell asleep. He didn't think he'd ever forget the sensation of having a trusting child curl up against him. He was glad no one was in the room to see his misty eyes. Careful so as not to wake her, he tucked Dee Dee into her bed and brushed a kiss over her forehead. It was cool; she was on the mend.

By early afternoon, Tim and Merry, though still confined to bed, were progressing nicely. Aunt Di had reached the point where she was regaining her appetite. Only Mike and Sharon were still running temperatures and suffering any queasiness.

The mighty bear was so weak Sam had had to half carry him back to his bed after his last bout of vomiting. If he'd had any doubt that Mike would recover quickly, it had dissolved when he'd told him he'd called Doug Bennett and informed him that his star running back was out of action for tonight's game. Mike hadn't offered even a token protest.

When Sam had looked in on Sharon the second time, she'd mumbled her thanks and gladly relinquished her family's care into his hands. He had taken her meek behavior as a sign of how sick she was. The Sharon he knew would have used every ounce of her remaining strength to take care of her kids; she obviously had none left.

Calling upon all he'd ever heard, read or experienced concerning the treatment of influenza, Sam had worked steadily to get Mike's and Sharon's temperatures down. He was proud of himself when, by late afternoon, his efforts were rewarded with cooler brows and less flushed faces.

Sam spent the early evening making sure all of his patients were resting comfortably. Throughout the day Theresa had been his able assistant. She had shown him where all the supplies were kept, and they'd taken turns doing laundry, soothing fevered brows and providing gallons of liquid for the infirm.

After the first couple of hours, the two of them had established a joking camaraderie that had made the drudgery easier. Theresa had complained, "Waiting on sick people is for the birds!"

"Then who better qualified than you and me?" Sam had quipped in return. "We bird-watchers are a hearty lot."

Theresa had immediately run up the stairs. "Where are you going?" Sam had called after her.

"To tell my brothers what you said," she called back over her shoulder. "They think bird-watchers are wimps, but they won't think so anymore. They believe anything you say."

She'd scampered up the stairs and left Sam to deal with the lump in his throat. How could he have doubted for a second that the rewards of being a parent far out-weighed the sacrifices? He could thrive for weeks on the compliment Theresa had just given him.

Over a simple supper, when all in the house were asleep except Sam and Theresa, she informed him of the names she'd given to each of their patients. "Mike's the vulture in the top nest—usually he eats anything," she related. "Tim's pretty smart, so I've been calling him an owl. Merry's in her loony stage, and Dee Dee's a baby robin because she's always got her mouth going."

Sam chuckled at Theresa's metaphoric appellations. "What have you come up with for Aunt Di?"

Theresa chewed a bite of the sandwich Sam had pre-pared for her before answering. "Well, I think she's a fallen swan, poor thing. Even sick, she's still graceful and regal."

Sam had a little different image of Diana. He would have labeled her an eagle. She was a very sharp-eyed, shrewd woman with an iron will and the strength of mind to soar beyond convention. Yet, she maintained an image of grace and beauty. Like the eagle, Diana Rhodes was a symbol of glory, and she was also an endangered species.

When he'd gone into her room, she'd been sitting up in bed, looking like the regal personage she was. She had lifted an imperious finger, waggled it at him and pronounced, "It's about time you came to your senses. I assume you'll be staying?"

Sam had gaped at her for a moment, then laughed. "You assume right, dear lady."

Diana had immediately closed her eyes, a smile playing about her lips. "A big family like ours needs a man. After the wedding I'll move out to the carriage house."

"Our family needs you, Diana," Sam had countered. "Under this roof."

Not even opening her eyes, she'd said, "True. See you in the morning, Sam."

Bringing his attention back to Theresa, Sam asked, "How about your mother?" He couldn't wait to hear her answer, wondering if it would come close to his own estimation.

"Mom's a little brown wren. She's content to stay in her nest and not bother anybody."

"Mmm," Sam murmured thoughtfully. "I don't think I see her that way. Wren's are plain little homebodies. Your mother's a nester, all right, but her plumage is hardly plain. In Mexico, I saw an *archilochus alexandri*, a beautiful hummingbird. That's how I see your mother. Like the females of that species, she can take care of her young without any help from a mate. She's a tiny, glittering creature who can fly circles around all of us."

Sam hadn't meant to give a speech, but he had a rapt audience. Theresa sighed. "That's beautiful. You really love my mom, don't you, Sam?"

"Very much, little cygnet," he responded with a smile. It was a relief to finally admit to someone how he felt—openly and honestly, without hesitation.

"You think of me as a baby swan?" she asked, wide-eyed and glowing.

"I sure do. You've got the soft, musical laughter of one, but you're no ugly duckling. You're already a beauty."

Theresa blushed in response to his compliment. "I wish I could marry you, but you're going to marry my mother," she announced with solemnity. "I'm glad I'm going to be your daughter, though. You're going to make a cool dad."

Sam was too shocked to respond. He had to look away. In the past ten hours he'd had to swallow several large lumps in his throat, but this was the biggest one yet. Theresa's unconditional confidence in his ability was a precious gift he would not dismiss lightly.

"I'm sure going to try," he finally choked out, acknowledging her assessment of his future role in her life. "I'll be very proud to have you as a daughter, but I think I'd better talk to your mom about marrying me before you make any announcements."

"Mike and Tim'll sure be glad. They weren't just talking about today when they said they were glad you were here," Theresa admitted. "All of us like you, and Mom's never sad when you're with her."

Sam didn't argue that last point even though it was far from the truth. Once, maybe, he'd made Sharon happy but he'd also hurt her, badly. He knew he'd been the cause of the dark shadows under her beautiful eyes, and the reason she no longer came to so many community events. She couldn't look at him without being overcome by sadness.

It had taken him two months of walking alone, questioning his values and reassessing what he wanted out of life, but he'd finally come to his senses. He hoped he could convince Sharon that he'd changed. Then he could end what he knew from personal experience was a continual, debilitating pain that cut deeper each day.

As much as he would have liked to go to Sharon right then and beg her to have him, he couldn't bring himself to take advantage of her in her weakened condition. When he proposed, he wanted her fully conscious and with strength enough to question the about-face he had taken on the subject of her children. She had every right to mistrust his motives for barging back into her life, but he was going to recant his previous philosophy so eloquently she'd have to believe him.

A week ago, even a day ago, he wouldn't have had the confidence to present a good case. However, in the past few hours he'd gone through a baptism by fire, and not only survived but had also been strengthened by the experience. This family had needed him today, and he'd risen to the challenge. He realized that the twenty-four-hour flu wasn't exactly a major crisis, but it had proved something to him. He was as capable as the next man of caring for those he loved.

Exhilarated by that knowledge, Sam carried on until well past midnight. Around ten o'clock, Theresa had begun to flag and he'd sent her to bed, concerned that she might become a flu victim if she didn't get some rest. Sam folded the last load of laundry, cleaned up the kitchen and checked on his patients one final time before giving in to his own fatigue. In Sharon's room he gazed down in contemplative silence at her sleeping form. She seemed peaceful, but to reassure himself that she was over the crisis, he gently laid his hand on her forehead. As all the others did, she now felt cool and normal. Unable to stop himself, he bent over and kissed her lightly, then tucked the blankets around her.

He switched off the lamp, but remained standing beside her bed. For a few seconds he considered going downstairs and sleeping on the couch. However, if he slept in the living room, he rationalized, he wouldn't hear if anyone called him. He chose to stay where he was. Sharon's bed looked soft, comfortable and plenty wide enough for the two of them. Stripping down to his briefs, he very quietly and carefully lifted the covers and slipped in beside her.

SHARON LIFTED her lids slowly, tentatively testing to make sure that when she focused her eyes, she'd see only one image. The room was nearly dark, but there was enough light coming through her open door from the hallway for her to make out the lamp on the table next to her. In the dimness she was able to discern that there was only one lamp, and it wasn't wavering or moving. Good, she deemed. Her temperature must be close to normal again.

Still curled up on her side, she took inventory of her body. Though her eyes still felt a little scratchy, they were working correctly. Her lips were dry, but her throat was no longer burning. Her head wasn't aching, though she wasn't yet ready to test it by lifting it up from the pillow. For now she'd be content to lie still and luxuriate in the lack of pain, hallucinations and stomach cramps.

She slowly began to straighten her legs. Only a slight ache remained, and her muscles didn't protest too much as she gathered her courage and stretched. It was over. She was back amongst the living.

According to her alarm clock, it wasn't quite five. She could catch a few more hours' sleep before the household awakened. Or maybe she'd sleep till noon, she decided, remembering that it was Saturday. Or maybe Sunday—she really wasn't sure how long she'd been sick. All she knew was that she'd never had a more violent case of the flu.

Her remembrance of the siege was fuzzy. They'd all been so very ill, with only Theresa to take care of them. No, not just Theresa. Someone else had been here. Someone Sharon had trusted. Someone who'd taken over and given them all tender, loving care. Sam.

Sharon smiled to herself in contentment. What a dear man Sam was. He hadn't turned tail and run, and the going couldn't have been rougher. If only...

Closing her eyes to savor the pleasant thought of Sam's being there, she rolled to her back and flung out her arms. Her hand hit warm, solid flesh. One of the children, no doubt. She pulled her arm back and turned her head on the pillow. "Sam!"

"I'm coming," he answered, instantly rolling out of bed and onto his feet. He started toward the doorway.

"Get back in here and close that door behind you," Sharon whispered tersely. She sat up and pulled the sheet to her chin. "You can't go traipsing around in...in your underwear."

With only a scrap of cotton riding low on his lean hips, Sam's virile body was prominently displayed. Sharon was sure the sight of him was more than her impressionable daughters should be subjected to. Aunt Di would have apoplexy. Even shaky and weak from her bout with the flu, Sharon was having trouble keeping her breathing steady and her libido in check.

Sam halted. "Nobody cares...they're too sick to care," he muttered, then shook his head to erase the grogginess. Semiawake, he looked back to the bed.

Even in the dim light, he could see Sharon's glaring expression. Eyes bright, her mouth set in a determined line, she was bristling. Obviously she'd recovered. Right then, he thought he preferred her sick and helpless.

Having determined that no one was in need of him, he closed the door and started back to the bed. The lamp on the opposite side came on as he lowered one knee on the mattress. "Don't you dare get in this bed!"

"Have a heart," Sam grumbled, too fatigued to think of anything beyond the moment. He'd run up and down three flights of stairs all day long and gotten up several times during the night to check on everyone. He'd had two hours of sleep at best and felt as if he'd been hit by a truck.

"I'm tired." He proceeded to climb into the bed. "Turn out that damned light," he snarled. Pulling the covers over his bare shoulders, he closed his eyes and nestled his head on the pillow.

Sharon started to fire off a negative retort, but stopped herself. Remembering how Sam had cared for her and her family, she felt instantly contrite. Begrudging the man his rest was small and mean. Instead of snapping at him, she should be thanking him.

She hadn't the slightest idea how he'd known of their plight, but like the calvary to the rescue, he'd arrived, taken over and saved them all. Considering the day he'd put in and her show of ingratitude, he had every right to snarl at her.

She turned off the light but his image remained in her mind. Sam's rumpled hair, the silvered temples more prominent, his face lined and pale. She lay back against her pillow. "Sam?" she called softly into the darkness.

"Yeah." His answer was low and sleepy sounding.

"I still love you."

"I know."

Sam reached across the bed and pulled Sharon into the curve of his body. Wrapping his arms around her and nestling her stacked-spoons fashion against him, he murmured, "Love you . . . kids . . . Aunt Di . . . now sleep."

His breathing was deep and even. Sharon had never heard anything more beautiful. She knew his being here, holding her in his arms was only temporary, but she meant to enjoy it while it lasted. Though she might have some fast explaining to do when her children discovered that Sam had spent the night in her bed, somehow she'd find the right words.

She wiggled slightly in an attempt to find a more comfortable position. Sam's arms tightened around her. She felt secure in his warmth, defended by the solid strength in him. Her mate was with her. With a sigh, Sharon closed her eyes and went back to sleep.

Hours later, she awakened again. She attempted to get up, but Sam's arms were still locked around her. Gently she pushed her elbow against his chest. "Sam..."

Her answer was the start of low snoring.

She tried again, her nudge a bit more forceful. "Sam."

The snoring stopped, but the arms around her didn't loosen one bit. "Sam. Let go of me."

"Never...never again," he muttered, shifting his legs. "You're all mine. I can do it."

Sharon twisted around in his arms until she was facing him. His eyes were still closed. A slight smile expanded his mouth.

His face wasn't flushed nor was his skin abnormally warm, so she knew his mutterings weren't fevered ramblings. Was it his subconscious talking? Or was he revealing his innermost thoughts as a result of a dream?

More awake and alert than she'd been in days, Sharon couldn't stand not knowing. She grabbed his shoulders and shook him. "Sam! What are you talking about?"

His eyes flew open, a startled expression on his face as he recognized her. Sharon's heart sank as Sam's arms dropped away. His declaration of not ever letting her go had been meaningless. She rolled away from him.

"Are you all right? Do you need anything?" he asked quickly. He propped himself up on his elbows.

"I...I'm fine," she managed, and slipping out of bed, she reached for a robe.

"You're sure?" He shook his head to clear it.

Sharon nodded as she tied the sash. Turning away, she put a few more feet between the bed and herself. With bright sunshine illuminating the room, she was painfully conscious of how terrible she must look.

She'd been too sick to care the day before, but now... She knew without checking that her hair was standing on end. It was little wonder the man had been startled when she'd awakened him. She was no doubt a fright!

"Get back in this bed," he ordered gruffly.

Sharon stood her ground. "I will not!"

She could understand that he'd crawled in with her when exhaustion had overtaken him last night. Yesterday hadn't been reality, but rather a terrible nightmare. With the new day and her recovery, things had to return to normal, which meant Sam was finished with his humanitarian duties.

Sam stared at her straight back and cursed himself for snapping at her. She wasn't a woman who took orders well. He knew that. He'd have to coax, persuade, convince, not bully.

Sharon took a step toward the door. "You're going to marry me," he blurted, forgetting all his good intentions. *Bravo, Jefferson! You really know how to turn on the sweet talk!*

Sharon whirled around in time to see the wince on Sam's face. "You're obviously too tired to know what you're saying. I'll forget you said that."

Sam bolted from the bed and in two strides was in front of her. "Don't forget it . . . please." He reached for her, but she took a step backward.

"Sorry," he said as he dropped his arms.

He looked so hurt, so devastated, Sharon could barely stand it. "Sam…I wish I could marry you." She gave him a bittersweet smile. "I do love you."

His expression brightened. "That's not all I need, sweetheart, not all I want."

Sharon frowned her puzzlement. "What are you trying to tell me?"

Carefully he slipped his arm around her waist, relieved that this time she didn't flinch. "I'm about to convince you to take a risk on me and let me share your life," he said, leading her to the plump, chintz-upholstered chair in the corner and gently urging her into it.

Sharon simply stared at Sam, her eyes huge and eloquent and hopeful.

"That's right," he confirmed. "I said share." He pulled the matching ottoman over and started to sit down. "I've got so much to say to you, Sharon."

"Uh . . . Sam?" Sharon stayed his progress downward. "Before we have a meaningful discussion would you grant me a favor?"

"Anything."

"Could I have five minutes in the bathroom?" she requested with a pleading grin.

He shoved the ottoman away and jumped out of her path. "You're sick again!"

"No, no," she protested with a giggle as she rose. "Just a little vanity."

On her way past her dresser, she grabbed up a hairbrush. At the doorway, she turned back to him. "I'd appreciate it if you'd put something on while I'm gone. Displaying so much of your gorgeous body is taking advantage of my weakened condition."

With that, she sailed through the doorway and down the hall, smiling as she heard him mutter, "I need all the advantages I can get."

In the bathroom Sharon took one look at herself and wasn't sure whether she should laugh or cry. She was a worse mess than she thought. Dark shadows stood under her eyes, and her hair stuck out in matted clumps. "The man can't be bedazzled by your looks," she muttered.

She stripped off her nightgown and stepped into the shower. In less than the five minutes she'd requested, she showered, shampooed her hair and brushed her teeth. Disdaining her nightgown, she opted for the fresher robe as her only garment. She towel-dried her short, curling hair as best she could. Even wet, it looked better than before.

Back in the bedroom, she found Sam standing by the window. His back was to her. He'd followed her suggestion and pulled on a pair of jeans and a T-shirt. She didn't find the addition of those muscle-hugging clothes helpful. He had a very distracting tush.

As if he could feel her eyes on him, Sam turned and smiled at her. "You didn't have to do that, you know. I've seen you looking worse."

Sharon closed the door behind her and leaned against it. "I guess you have."

She felt more self-conscious now than she'd felt in her disheveled state moments ago. She knew good and well what they were about to discuss. The only mystery was why he'd finally realized what everyone else already knew: that he would make the perfect father for her children and the perfect husband for her.

From opposite sides of the room, they faced each other. Sharon was ready to say anything to break the silence when Sam swore impatiently. "Hell, I don't know any other way of going about this. I love you, and I can't stand the way we've been apart these past few months. I'm sick to death of living in the backyard."

His lower lip came out with belligerence. "I'm over in the big house now, and I'm not leaving." The next second, all belligerence was gone. "Is that okay with you?"

"Sure is," Sharon confirmed saucily as she advanced on him. Coming to a stop a few feet away, she continued. "Of course, this is a pretty big deal. Maybe you don't realize what you're getting into. You're a lawyer. If you want to, you could still argue your way out of this with some fancy legal talk."

Sam let out a disgusted snort. "Temporary insanity is the only plea I can make for not contracting for the whole package the first time. For punishment, I deserve a life sentence."

"At hard labor? That's what you're asking for if you take us all on. Sure you're up to it?"

"I did pretty well during the plague," he announced smugly.

"You were wonderful," she complimented sincerely. "That was rough, but sometimes it gets a lot rougher. You have to be willing to say no when it would be a lot easier to say yes. You have to be flexible enough to give a kid time that you've been looking forward to spending alone. You have to—"

"Love them," he finished for her. He pulled her into his arms. "Sam Jefferson, swinging single, is begging you to put him on the family plan and end his misery."

"Oh Sam, I've been miserable, too."

"But no longer." He held her close, rocking back and forth, his cheek resting on the top of her head. "I already talked to Diana, and she agrees I should move in here right away."

Leaning back against the arms encircling her, Sharon asked, "What are you going to do with the carriage house? After all the work you've done, it can't go empty."

"That's where we'll go when I've been given time off for good behavior." He gave her a hard squeeze. "How does that sound?"

"Wonderful." She slipped her arms around his neck and pulled his face downward for her kiss.

The pledge was made with tenderness, passion and love—an all-encompassing boundless love. As their lips parted for breath, Sam said triumphantly, "I sure missed this part of the package deal."

"You'll never have to again." Sharon began to lead him back to bed.

Sam went willingly, tugging the sash of her robe open as they fell upon the mattress. His large hands closed over her breasts, and Sharon pressed closer as his lips took possession of hers again. Her entire body seemed to be on fire, her nerves tingling wherever he touched. She hadn't dared hope, but now all her dreams had come true.

"I love you," she whispered, treasuring the words as she treasured the man. "Love me, Sam. Please, now."

"Oh no." Sam's voice was a weak moan. "Not now."

"Why not?" Sharon asked in disbelief.

"I'm so sorry, my darling," he groaned. "But I think I'm going to be sick."

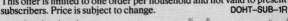

Harlequin "Super Celebration"
SWEEPSTAKES

NEW PRIZES—NEW PRIZE FEATURES & CHOICES—MONTHLY

1. To enter the sweepstakes, follow the instructions outlined on the Center Insert Card. Alternate means of entry, NO PURCHASE NECESSARY, you may also enter by mailing your name, address and birthday on a plain 3″ x 5″ piece of paper to: In U.S.A.: Harlequin "Super Celebration" Sweepstakes, P.O. Box 1867, Buffalo, N.Y. 14240-1867. In Canada: Harlequin "Super Celebration" Sweepstakes, P.O. Box 2800, 5170 Yonge Street, Postal Station A, Willowdale, Ontario M2N 6J3.

2. Winners will be selected in random drawings from all entries received. All prizes will be awarded. These prizes are in addition to any free gifts which might be offered. Versions of this sweepstakes with different prizes may appear in other presentations by TorStar and their affiliates. The maximum value of the prizes offered is $8,000.00. Winners selected will receive the prize offered from their prize package.

3. The selection of winners will be conducted under the supervision of Marden-Kane, an independent judging organization. By entering the sweepstakes, each entrant accepts and agrees to be bound by these rules and the decision of the judges which shall be final and binding. Odds of winning are dependent upon the total number of entries received. Taxes, if any, are the sole responsibility of the winners. Prizes are not transferable. This sweepstakes is scheduled to appear in Retail Outlets of Harlequin Books during the period of June 1986 to December 1986. All entries must be received by January 31st, 1987. The drawing will take place on or about March 1st, 1987 at the offices of Marden-Kane, Lake Success, New York. For Quebec (Canada) residents, any litigation regarding the running of this sweepstakes and the awarding of prizes must be submitted to La Regie de Lotteries et Course du Quebec.

4. This presentation offers the prizes as illustrated on the Center Insert Card.

5. This offer is open to residents of the U.S., and Canada, 18 years or older, except employees of TorStar, its affilliates, subsidiaries, Marden-Kane and all other agencies and persons connected with conducting this sweepstakes. All Federal, State and local laws apply. Void where prohibited or restricted by law. Winners will be notified by mail and may be required to execute an affidavit of eligibility and release which must be returned within 14 days after notification. Winners consent to the use of their name, photograph and/or likeness for advertising and publicity in conjunction with this and similar promotions without additional compensation. One prize per family or household. Canadian winners will be required to answer a skill testing question.

6. For a list of our most recent prize winners, send a stamped, self-addressed envelope to: WINNERS LIST, c/o Marden-Kane, P.O. Box 525, Sayreville, NJ 08872.

No Lucky Number needed to win!

Janet Dailey

Americana

A romantic tour of America with Janet Dailey!

Enjoy the first two releases of this collection of your favorite previously published Janet Dailey titles, presented alphabetically state by state.

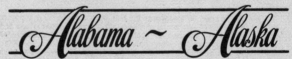

Alabama ~ Alaska

Available in June wherever paperback books are sold or reserve your copy for May shipping by sending your name, address and zip or postal code, along with a check or money order for $2.75 per book (plus 75¢ for postage and handling) payable to Harlequin Reader Service to:

Harlequin Reader Service

In the U.S.
901 Fuhrmann Blvd.
P.O. Box 1397
Buffalo, NY 14240

In Canada
P.O. Box 2800
Postal Station A
5170 Yonge Street
Willowdale, Ont. M2N 6J3

JDA-A-IRRR